"Lucas, look out!" Paige shrieked.

As he swung his gaze back to the road, Lucas's heart slammed against his rib cage. He stomped on the brakes, causing the front tire to screech on the wet pavement. The minivan came to a halt, inches from where the heavy rains had washed out a chunk of the road.

There was no going forward. He would have to turn the minivan around and go back.

A car came around the bend in the road.

The dark blue sedan that had been parked behind the gas station.

The car stopped several yards from them, and a man climbed out. There was no mistaking the ghastly snowy hair and skin of Colin Richter.

Fear jolted through Lucas. They were trapped. The road was gone in front of them, and the bridge was down behind them. Frantic to protect his charges, he said, "We have to get out and make a run for it into the woods."

Paige let out an audible gasp. "That's him! The man who wants to kill me."

Terri Reed's romance and romantic suspense novels have appeared on the *Publishers Weekly* top twenty-five and NPD BookScan top one hundred lists and have been featured in *USA TODAY*, *Christian Fiction* magazine and *RT Book Reviews*. Her books have been finalists for the Romance Writers of America RITA® Award and the National Readers' Choice Award and finalists three times for the American Christian Fiction Writers Carol Award. Contact Terri at terrireed.com or PO Box 19555, Portland, OR 97224.

Books by Terri Reed

Love Inspired Suspense

Buried Mountain Secrets
Secret Mountain Hideout
Christmas Protection Detail
Secret Sabotage
Forced to Flee
Forced to Hide
Undercover Christmas Escape
Shielding the Innocent Target

Rocky Mountain K-9 Unit

Detection Detail

Pacific Northwest K-9 Unit

Explosive Trail

Visit the Author Profile page at LoveInspired.com for more titles.

Shielding the Innocent Target

TERRI REED

LOVE INSPIRED SUSPENSE
INSPIRATIONAL ROMANCE

LOVE INSPIRED® SUSPENSE
INSPIRATIONAL ROMANCE

ISBN-13: 978-1-335-59812-7

Shielding the Innocent Target

Recycling programs
for this product may
not exist in your area.

Love Inspired
22 Adelaide St. West, 41st Floor
Toronto, Ontario M5H 4E3, Canada
www.LoveInspired.com

Printed in Lithuania

MIX
Paper | Supporting
responsible forestry
FSC® C021394

Delight thyself also in the Lord:
and he shall give thee the desires of thine heart.
—*Psalm* 37:4

To my daughter—
you are a delight and a gift from God.

ONE

"You'll do what you're told. It's very simple."

The unfamiliar female voice froze Paige Walsh in her boss's office doorway. The threat in the unseen woman's tone was unmistakable.

A shiver of unease cascaded down Paige's spine and she nearly dropped the manila mail envelope she carried. She resisted the urge to peek around the half-open door leading into the expansive corner office on the top floor of the downtown Fort Meyers Southwest Professional Building.

Working late was normal for Paige and her boss.

But having visitors after-hours certainly was unusual.

From where Paige stood, she could see her boss, Federal Prosecutor Donald Lessing, standing behind his mahogany desk. The floor-to-ceiling windows running the length of the wall revealed the darkened sky.

Who was the woman? What was happening?

"You won't get away with this," Donald stated, his voice quivering with a note of fear. His gaze darted to Paige. He gave a shake of his head before he returned his focus to his visitor. "I won't let you."

"Then you leave us no choice."

Paige frowned. Should she intervene? Did her boss need her help?

She took a step forward just as a man, dressed all in

black with a shocking head of white hair and pale skin, appeared in Paige's line of sight.

He held a gun aimed at Donald's heart.

Shocked, Paige's pulse spiked. A wave of dizziness washed over her. This couldn't be happening.

Donald held up his hands. "Please, don't do this."

The gunman squeezed the trigger. A barely there, popping noise burst from the barrel of the wicked-looking weapon.

Blood bloomed across the front of her boss's chest.

Paige's gasp rang as loud as a shotgun blast to her ears.

The murderer whirled to face her, his pale blue eyes locking with hers. Dead eyes. She'd never understood the term—until now. He had a red angry scar running from his left temple down to his neck.

Fear, feral and ominous, snatched the breath from Paige's lungs.

From the other side of the office door, the woman ordered, "Get her. You can't let her leave."

It was all the impetus Paige needed to give in to the flight response clamoring through her system. Clutching the manila mail envelope to her chest, she raced down the hallway toward the elevator. The terrorizing sound of pounding feet chasing her made her stomach contract and nausea rise to burn her throat.

If he trapped her in the elevator she would never survive. What would happen to her son?

She bypassed the elevator and ran for the emergency stairwell. She flung the door open hard enough to bounce it against the concrete wall. She charged down the steps, one hand gripping the rail to prevent her from falling face-first. Her heels clattered with every quaking step.

The man entered the stairwell behind her, rapidly closing the distance between them.

Panic flared hot, searing her insides. Her shoes were slowing her down. With a practiced maneuver, she kicked the heels off and continued barefoot down the rest of the fourteen flights of stairs to the lobby. The concrete scraped against the tender soles of her feet.

Faster! Faster! The word ricocheted through her mind. *Oh, Lord, please, let me get away.*

She heard that same barely there popping noise and the concrete wall beside her head erupted with bits of debris hitting her in the face. She screamed and hunched as she reached the lobby door. Still clutching the manila envelope, she pushed through the door, rounded a corner, and ran to the security desk at the front of the building.

Two security guards sat unconcerned in front of video monitors. Why hadn't they seen what was happening?

"I don't understand it," one of the guards she knew as Sean said. "Something's messing with the—"

"Help! Help, my boss has been shot." Paige skidded to a halt at the desk.

The older guard, Edward, came out from behind the desk and gripped her by the shoulders. "Get ahold of yourself. Explain."

"Someone shot my boss. The gunman chased me down the stairwell. Call the police!"

"On it." Sean picked up the landline phone.

"Who's your boss?" Edward asked.

"Federal Prosecutor Donald Lessing."

Paige's breathing puffed out in gasps and her heart thumped wildly in her chest. Cold from the marble floor seeped into the soles of her feet. Expecting the murderer to come blasting around the corner at any moment, she inched her way behind the security guard, unconsciously using him as a shield.

Moments passed before the wail of sirens filled the

lobby and bounced off the marble flooring and mahogany paneling.

A swarm of police officers hurried inside. A uniformed female officer approached along with an older plainclothes detective who flashed his badge. "Detective Finley. What's going on here?"

"Our security cameras are down." Edward pointed to Paige. "She claims her boss has been shot."

Claims? "I'm Paige Walsh. I'm a paralegal for Federal Prosecutor Donald Lessing." Frustration laced her words. "We were working late. I went to his office—" She swallowed as the memory of the blood spreading across Donald's chest reared its head, making her dizzy. "There were people in his office. A woman and a man. The man he—he shot Donald. He chased me down the emergency stairwell."

Where was he? Had he given up?

But she'd seen him.

She could identify him.

That meant he had to eliminate her.

Her throat closed. Her stomach pitched again.

The assailants could be hiding anywhere. He could find her office and discover her name and where she lived.

Her father had warned her that working for a federal prosecutor could be dangerous. But she'd never really believed it. The situation was so surreal. Why would someone want to hurt Donald?

She nearly scoffed aloud. There were any number of people who would want a federal prosecutor out of the picture. Donald was aggressive. He didn't play games and he was honest. The very reasons she had grown to admire and respect him.

"What floor?" Detective Finley asked.

Focusing on the policeman, she took a breath. "Fourteen. Suite fifteen." Paige grabbed the detective's sleeve before he could move. "I need my purse from my office. Suite thirteen."

Finley nodded. "I'll see what I can do." With a posse of armed uniformed officers, he led the way to the elevator and disappeared while several more officers took the stairwell.

Paige glanced at the female officer standing expectantly beside her. Noting the name badge, Paige said, "Officer Alonso, I need to get to my son. He's at a home day care." And then she was going to get as far from Florida as possible.

"I need you to answer some questions first," the officer said as she pulled a small notebook out of her pocket. "Why were you and your boss working late? Is this something you did often?"

The suspicion in her eyes grated along Paige's nerves. "We weren't having an affair if that's what you're suggesting. Donald was working on opening arguments for a trial that starts tomorrow. He asked if I could do some last-minute research."

The officer wrote down her answer. "What can you tell me about the people who were in the office?"

"The woman seemed to be in charge, but I didn't see her. The shooter—" Paige swallowed the bile burning her throat. "He was—" She searched for the words to describe him. "He looked like the undead."

Officer Alonso's gaze widened. "Excuse me?"

"You know, like in those TV shows and video games about zombies," Paige replied. She'd often caught her son trying to sneak a peek at them. "The man was pale. Unnaturally pale. White hair. Piercing pale blue eyes. Wearing all black. And he has a scar on the left side of his face."

The officer's eyebrows rose. "That does sound like something from a horror movie. Do you think he was wearing makeup?"

The question gave her pause. Was it all just an effect to hide his identity? "Possibly. I don't know."

"What can you tell me about the gun?" the officer asked.

With a shudder, Paige replied, "Big. Black. It didn't make much noise."

"Interesting." She wrote in the notebook. "It had a noise suppressor."

Dropping her chin in surprise, Paige asked, "Like one used by professional hit men?"

"Do you know any professional hit men?"

Paige could tell the woman was trying not to smile. "Of course not. Just what I see on television or read in books." Paige loved to read thriller novels. The assassins always had silencers on their weapons. Anxiety twisted in her gut. This was bad.

Detective Finley returned and handed over her large satchel that served as a purse.

She slipped the envelope inside and hitched the strap over her shoulder. "Is my boss...?" Paige grimaced. "Did he make it?"

"I'm sorry," the detective replied with a shake of his head.

A pang of grief stabbed her. She wasn't a stranger to sorrow. After losing her husband and then her mother, she understood that life was short and could end in a blink.

"The office was ransacked." Detective Finley drew her attention. "Any idea what the gunman was looking for?"

"No. I could look to see if anything is missing..." she offered, though the thought of returning to the scene of the crime gripped her with dread.

"This is a federal case because Donald Lessing was a federal employee," the detective said. "They will be taking over as soon as they arrive. Once the victim is removed, the feds might take you up on the offer." He focused on Officer

Alonso. "Take her to the station. The FBI are going to want to talk to her. They can bring her back later."

"Wait," Paige said. "I need to get my son." She was thankful she'd taken the bus into work today and wouldn't be leaving her minivan parked in the garage. She tried to use public transportation occasionally to cut down on parking fees.

The officer hooked her hand around Paige's elbow and tugged her toward the building exit. "We'll stop on the way."

Grateful, Paige allowed the officer to escort her to the police cruiser parked at the curb. She slid into the back seat while the officer climbed in front and used the radio to tell dispatch she was bringing in a witness.

She turned to stare at Paige through the bulletproof glass separating the front and back seats. "Address?"

Paige sat forward and told her the home day care's location. She settled back and buckled up, but she couldn't shake the unease sliding through her veins and making her skin crawl. She'd seen the killer. The image of the man popped up in her mind like a spooky jack-in-the-box clown. She prayed she wouldn't be harmed by the burden of witnessing a murder.

The police cruiser peeled away from the building and headed down the street. The downtown traffic was minimal. As they wound their way through the city toward the residential area of Whiskey Creek, Paige worked hard to steady her breathing. She didn't want to alarm her son. Her hands still shook, her fingers cold. She lifted a prayer for this nightmare to be over.

Suddenly the police officer sped up.

Paige's heart thumped. "What's going on?"

"This is Officer Alonso," she said into her radio. "Requesting backup. I'm being followed and they are coming up fast." She gave the address of where they were. To Paige, she said, "Brace yourself. They're going to hit us."

As the words left the officer's mouth, there was a jarring impact at the back of the vehicle. Paige's teeth rattled in her head. The patrol car rotated in a wide circle. The tires screeched on the pavement. Paige screamed and grabbed the door handle. The side of the cruiser slammed into a tree planted in the green space of the median strip separating the south and northbound lanes.

Gasping for breath, she fought to gain her equilibrium.

In the front seat, Officer Alonso was slumped against the window.

Paige banged her fist against the glass. "Wake up. Wake up."

The back window exploded. A shower of glass rained down on Paige. She screamed and worked to unbuckle the seat belt. There was no door handle. There was no mechanism for her to disengage the lock. She was trapped inside the car with an assassin on her tail.

She scrunched down as small as she could on the floorboard and dug out her cell phone from her purse. She dialed 911.

"Come on," she muttered as the phone rang.

The door handle above her head rattled. Someone was trying to get in.

Another blast of glass rained down on Paige as the back passenger-side door window exploded. Startled, she dropped the phone.

A rough hand grabbed her by the hair, yanking her up and trying to pull her out of the car. She screamed and grabbed onto the seat belt to anchor herself in the car.

"Just kill her already," that same female voice said from outside the car.

Paige's heart contracted painfully in her chest. *Lord,*

please! Please, you can't let me die. Kenny can't lose both of his parents.

The wail of sirens rent the air. The screech of tires on pavement brought the hope of rescue.

The man released his hold on Paige's hair. She scrambled away to the other side of the back seat. She heard the popping noise of the gun. A searing pain lanced across the top of her shoulder. Had she been shot? *Please, Lord, I don't want to die. I can't leave Kenny alone.*

Deputy US Marshal Lucas "Caveman" Cavendish entered his boss's office in the San Antonio headquarters of the US Marshal service. Marshal Gavin Armstrong nodded his silver-haired head and gestured to the captain seat across the desk from him.

"Am I in trouble?" Lucas asked, half-joking. Wasn't often he was called into the boss's office in the late hours of the evening. He swept the tan cowboy hat off his head and crossed one booted ankle over his knee.

"Not in the least." Gavin's deep gravelly voice rubbed around Lucas as if sanding down the edges.

There was something about Gavin that put people at ease. Just one of the things that made him such a great marshal and boss. Some speculated he would retire soon. Lucas hoped they were false rumors.

"I need you to bring a witness here while a relocation package is put together." He slid a file folder across the desk.

Lucas bit back a groan. He preferred tactical operations and fugitive investigations. The more active roles within the marshal's service. He liked taking down the bad guys. Not babysitting witnesses.

But he had no intention of doing anything to tank his

career. This job was everything to him. He picked up the file folder and flipped it open.

The photo of a woman dressed in a professional business suit stared up at him with large luminous blue eyes. Her strawberry blond hair was pulled back into a severe bun. But it was the killer smile that grabbed his attention. "What'd she do?"

Gavin arched an eyebrow. "So jaded." He shook his head. "Paige Walsh witnessed her boss's murder."

Okay. Not a criminal. Setting the file back on the desk, Lucas asked, "Why me?"

"The victim is Federal Prosecutor Donald Lessing."

Stunned as recognition flared, he dropped his raised foot to the ground with a thud. "He's the one prosecuting Adam Wayne."

"Yes. He was."

Rising, Lucas paced while his hands worried the brim of his cowboy hat. "What will this mean for the trial?"

"It's been postponed."

Anger burned low in his gut. "For how long?"

"Until the situation can be sorted," Gavin said.

Pausing, he stared at his boss. "Sorted? What does that mean?" Lucas slapped his hat against his thigh. "Another prosecutor can take over, right?"

"There seems to be an issue with the files."

Unbelievable. "An issue?"

"They are missing along with Lessing's computer."

Dread pinched his lungs. "Isn't everything in the cloud?"

"As I said, issues. The FBI has their best techs on it."

Pressure like an anvil settled on Lucas's chest. His body vibrated with tension. *God, why is this happening?* "It took nearly two years for the task force to gather enough intel to bring down Wayne and cripple his empire." The arms dealer had been as slippery as a viper and just as deadly.

"Indeed," Gavin replied. "And now they've assassinated the prosecutor and stolen the files. They've already tried to eliminate the witness. She and her son need protection."

Lucas sat back down. He hated the idea of a child in danger. The weight of responsibility to make the world a safer place sat heavy on his shoulders. A calling he'd felt God leading him to from a young age and had kept him from forming any romantic attachments. It was easier to hunt bad guys without the additional worry of his job impacting someone else's life. "What about the kid's father?"

"Deceased." Gavin steepled his hands.

"Does Barlow know?" Lucas referred to his former boss and task force leader, Homeland Security Agent James Barlow, recently promoted to the head of the Transnational Organized Crime Mission Center.

"I'd imagine he's been informed," Gavin replied.

"I'll check in with him if that's okay with you?" Lucas didn't want to commit a faux pas. Gavin was his boss now, but Lucas held James in high esteem and felt a sense of loyalty to the man.

"A good idea. Agent Barlow will want to be kept in the loop," Gavin said. "However, there's more."

More? Lucas wasn't sure he wanted to hear more. Absorbing the information that the case against Adam Wayne could be in jeopardy was hard enough.

The verse in Romans played through his mind. *In all things God works for the good of those who love Him.*

But sometimes life wasn't good or just. And reconciling the promises of the Bible to reality made faith so much more difficult and necessary.

"From the witness's description, the killer sounds like the man you nicknamed The Beast."

Shock stole Lucas's breath. After a heartbeat, he managed to say, "He's dead."

"Apparently, you're not the only one who faked his death," Gavin stated in a grim tone that skated along Lucas's flesh.

If The Beast, aka Colin Richter, was gunning for Paige Walsh and her son, Lucas would do everything in his power to keep them out of the line of fire.

And the burning desire to bring down Colin and make sure Adam Wayne went to prison for a very long time wouldn't be denied. The only way to accomplish what needed to be done was to return to Florida. "When do I leave?"

Paige's flesh burned where the bullet had grazed the top of her shoulder. She still couldn't believe she'd survived the attempt on her life. The sirens had scared the assassin and his boss off.

Paige had been rushed by ambulance to the hospital where she received a dressing over the wound. She'd refused the pain medication. She needed to keep a clear head. The FBI had told her the Wayne file was missing along with Donald's computer, and her own computer had been destroyed. She'd given the FBI access to the cloud information but apparently there was some sort of corruption in the data, and they were working on recovering the information.

Her heart rate was still too high and her blood pressure elevated, but at least she and her son were safe in the conference room of the Fort Meyers Police Department. Someone had found a coloring book and crayons for her six-year-old. His blond head was bent as he worked to color in the lines with a blue crayon. The color nearly matching the blue of his eyes.

At their feet lay Kenny's therapy dog, Aslan. The huge golden retriever sensed Paige's agitation. From the moment Kenny, dressed in a clean red collared shirt and jeans, and

Aslan, wearing his therapy vest, had arrived via police escort, the dog had been attentive to both her and Kenny.

Thankfully, the police had allowed his home day care provider, Mrs. Gardner, to accompany Kenny to the police station. She'd fussed over Paige when she'd arrived, but for her own safety, the police had returned her home.

After being interviewed by the FBI and now left alone in the conference room with her son and the dog, Paige needed to make plans. God had watched over her today. She prayed He would continue to do so. As soon as she could gain access to a computer, she would figure out how to get her, Kenny and Aslan to Germany. After her mother's death, her father had returned to his home country.

They should be safe far from Florida. At least she prayed so.

A disturbance in the outer portion of the police department had her heart jumping into her throat. There was no yelling or shouting, just a tangible tension that reached her and ratcheted up her nerves.

She glanced out the door of the conference room and locked eyes with a tall cowboy. He had brown wavy hair visible beneath a tan cowboy hat, deep brown eyes that stared at her intently and a five-o'clock shadow highlighting his strong square jaw. He was dressed in jeans and a white button-down shirt beneath a leather jacket that emphasized the breadth of his wide shoulders.

Her heart bumped against her chest as attraction zinged through her veins. She couldn't remember the last time she'd reacted to someone so viscerally. It must be the shock of seeing her boss murdered and almost being killed herself. She gave herself a mental shake.

The man strode toward her with long confident strides, while the special agent from the FBI and the police chief followed in his wake.

Paige shifted, blocking her son from the man's view. Who was he? What did he want? She dug into her purse, grabbing her phone and a pair of headphones. She urged Kenny to put the headphones in his ears and played his favorite music, the soundtrack to a children's film.

Awareness shimmied over her skin. On a breath, she turned to find herself staring into the warm chocolate eyes of the cowboy.

"Ma'am." He touched the brim of his cowboy hat and dipped his chin. "I'm Deputy US Marshal Lucas Cavendish. I'm here to escort you to San Antonio."

"What?" Nobody told her they were moving her to Texas.

"It's in your best interest to allow the US Marshals to protect you and your son." He stepped to the side so that he could see Kenny.

Paige shifted again, blocking his view. "What exactly does that mean?"

Lucas returned his focus to her. The urge to squirm under that intense regard was nearly impossible to resist, but resist she did. She knew she looked frightful. Her bun had come loose and now was held back by a scrunchie she'd found in her satchel. Her blouse was bloodied, and she wore hospital slippers.

"Relocation. New identities," Lucas said calmly. "You'll be safe so you can testify in court once the killer is brought to justice."

She shook her head. "I'd rather take Kenny and go overseas. My father lives in Munich. We would be safe there."

With a negative shake of his head, Lucas said, "Not from this man, you won't."

The surety in his voice caused a cascade of unease to ripple down her back. "What makes you so sure?"

"You'll have to trust me," Lucas stated.

"Trust you?" That was a lot to ask. Trust didn't come easily. It had to be earned.

Something flashed in Lucas's eyes, but she couldn't discern the emotion.

"The quicker we get you relocated the better," he told her. "You worked on the Wayne case, correct?"

"I did." Her heart thumped with anxiety. "Why can't we go to Munich where my father lives?"

"The man who killed your boss will stop at nothing to make sure you can't testify against him or reveal anything you know about the Wayne case. He's a vicious killer with no regard for life."

A lump of dread formed in her throat. She forced herself to ask, "And you know this how?"

"Because I'm the one who put that scar on his face."

The words reverberated through her head. The marshal had gone up against the killer and survived. Did she dare trust he would be able to keep her and Kenny alive?

TWO

FBI Special Agent Brandon McIntosh took a seat across from Paige, drawing her attention away from the handsome deputy US marshal.

McIntosh was an older man with light brown hair going gray at the temples. "Mrs. Walsh, I know this is scary for you," he said. "And for your son. But this is what the US Marshals do. It would help us greatly if you entered witness protection while we conduct a manhunt for the assassin."

"You don't have any guarantee that you'll find him." She hated the way her voice trembled.

She didn't want these men to think her weak. Why did she have to go through this?

The Bible said to rejoice in trials of many kinds. She had a hard time believing God meant something like the murder of her boss.

Kenny put down his crayon and removed the earbuds from his ears. Aslan settled his chin on her knee.

"Mommy," Kenny said, his bright blue eyes meeting hers as he reached to grip her hand. "I want to go with the cowboy."

He'd heard the conversation. Her stomach sank. Of course, he wanted to go with the man dressed like a cowboy. Kenny was fascinated with the Wild West. "He's not a real cowboy, honey. He's a US marshal."

"I beg to differ, ma'am," Lucas said, tipping his hat again. "Before I joined the Marine Corps and the US Marshals, I worked the rodeo circuit." He winked at Kenny. "I can bring a bull to heel and sit a bucking bronc just fine."

He was a marine. And US marshal. A man committed to serving his country. She didn't want to admit she was impressed. "How long will this take?"

Lucas sat down next to her, crowding her space, but there was nowhere for her to go. "Giving your witness statement or WITSEC?"

"Both."

"As long as it takes."

Aslan popped up from under the table, pushing himself between her and the cowboy. She buried her fingers into his fur, grateful for his unexpected protection. The big golden retriever was trained to detect Kenny's epileptic seizures, not to be a guard dog. Yet, he'd known she needed his intervention. She'd bought Aslan from a service dog organization when he was a year old, just after Kenny was diagnosed at age three.

One side of Lucas's mouth lifted, and his expression softened. What would a real smile do to his handsome face? Why did she even care?

"Good job," he said to Aslan and held out his hand, palm down for the dog to sniff.

Aslan snuffled his nose against the man's very strong capable-looking hand. Lucas turned his palm up, revealing calluses. The hands of a cowboy.

Surprisingly, Aslan put his large paw onto the man's palm as if shaking his hand.

Paige frowned in surprise. She'd never seen Aslan behave that way with anyone. Was the dog giving his stamp of approval? Should she go with the marshal? What choice did she have? She, and Kenny by extension, were in danger.

The thought of going it alone filled her with dread.

Yet, she'd been alone for a long time. Relying on someone else, especially a handsome intimidating man, wasn't ideal. But the threat of murder was a strong motivator. She'd do what she had to in order to keep Kenny safe.

But trusting the attractive cowboy marshal? That would be a feat.

"I'll need to go to my house to pack a bag and pick up Kenny's medications."

Lucas nodded. "A trip to your home can be arranged."

Lucas climbed out of the SUV and stood still for a moment, letting his senses take in the surroundings. Nothing struck a warning on his internal alert system. No out-of-place noise, no one about at this early morning hour. The sun's rays were just breaking over the horizon, bathing the world in a warm spring glow. He swiveled to take in the bungalow-style house with a wide expanse of lawn.

A swing set and slide were off to the side of the house. A large doghouse with the name Aslan painted in blue over the opening butted up against the side. A driveway led to a garage around the back. He wasn't sure what he'd expected. Maybe something more formal for the paralegal working for a federal prosecutor, but this house was inviting. Homey.

He opened the SUV's back door for Paige to exit. When Kenny and Aslan made to follow her out, he held up a hand. "You two stay put." He met the gaze of FBI Special Agent McIntosh in the driver's seat of the SUV.

"I've got them," McIntosh said.

Lucas gave a nod and urged Paige to get inside.

The interior was even cozier. Light-colored walls covered with landscape photographs and gleaming blond hardwood floors created an airy space. There were toys for both the child and the dog scattered about on the floor. The place looked lived in.

A comfy houndstooth-patterned sofa faced the TV, which was flanked by two bookshelves filled with what appeared to be law books, children's books and fiction books. He could see through an archway a dining space with a sideboard and a kitchen with white tile and blue accents.

Paige moved to go down the hallway.

"Wait," Lucas told her. "I need to make sure we're alone."

"But—"

He dipped his chin and gave her a look that had her clamping her lips together. She huffed out a breath and nodded. Keeping the urge to smile at her irritation from showing, he placed a hand on his sidearm and moved deeper into the house.

Stepping over a rawhide bone, Lucas walked down the short hallway. He checked the two bedrooms and bath to make sure no one hid, waiting to pounce. He smiled at the boy's race car–themed decor and the very feminine bedroom that reminded him of his middle sister's. Frilly and flowered. But he felt like an intruder in Paige's private space.

Back in the living room, he closed the curtains on the front window. "We're good."

"Deputy."

Paige's voice vibrated with anxiety and drew him away from the living room into the dining room.

She stood staring, transfixed, at the table.

He stepped to her side and sucked in a breath.

A gun with a silencer attached to the barrel lay on top of a coloring book.

Dread and apprehension raced through him. Colin had been here. There was no doubt in Lucas's mind that this was the weapon used to kill the federal prosecutor.

The gun had been left as a threat.

A warning that Paige would be next. And it wasn't a coincidence Colin left the gun on her son's coloring book. Kenny was in danger, too.

"We need to get out of here," he said.

"But I have to pack bags. And get Kenny's medication." Paige pivoted and headed toward the hallway.

"Grab the meds but don't touch anything else," he told her. "We have to wait for the crime scene unit to check the house for any trace evidence."

Her blue eyes searched his face. "Do you honestly think they'll find anything?"

Acid churned in his gut. "Probably not." Colin was careful. He wouldn't leave anything behind. That he'd left a witness alive was sloppy and unlike the efficient hired assassin Lucas knew him to be. "But it's protocol."

She grabbed what she needed.

Urging her back to the SUV, he filled McIntosh in on the situation and called the police chief.

While they waited for more police presence and the crime scene unit van to arrive, Lucas called Gavin and then James Barlow, filling both men in on the situation and the plan to take a JPATS plane out of Florida. It was odd feeling the pressure to report to two bosses.

Over two hours later, the crime scene techs took the murder weapon, put it in a bag and released the house.

Once again, Lucas helped Paige out of the SUV, but this time released Kenny and Aslan from the vehicle so they could stretch their legs. McIntosh stayed with them.

Lucas and Paige went inside, and Paige immediately walked down the hallway. He followed her. She entered Kenny's bedroom. Race car bed, race car posters on the wall. He recognized a couple of characters from an animated children's movie. Paige hurried to grab a duffel bag from the closet and stuffed clothes inside.

"You could help," Paige said. "By going to the hall closet and grabbing a duffel bag to pack with Aslan's things."

Leaning against the doorjamb, he shook his head. "I'm not leaving your side."

She rolled her eyes and zipped up the duffel, then shoved it into his chest as she walked past him. "You can be the Sherpa."

"Yes, ma'am," Lucas said. "That I can do."

In her bedroom, he stayed on the threshold as Paige took a small rolling suitcase from the closet and laid it open on the flowered comforter covering the bed. She went to the dresser and paused. She turned to face him. "I'd really like for you to step into the hall and wait."

"I have three sisters," Lucas told her.

"I'm not your sister." She shooed him away with her hand. "Go on."

He couldn't argue with her on that score. He was keenly aware of this woman's beauty and quiet strength. Pivoting, he stepped out of the bedroom and leaned against the wall. He could hear her moving around, opening and closing drawers and the sliding door of the closet.

She entered the hall with the rolling carry-on suitcase and parked it next to him before she proceeded into the bathroom. Several moments later, she emerged with a bag filled with toiletries.

He took the toiletries bag, which was heavier than he'd expected, and hooked it to the carry-on before following her back to the living room. She pulled another duffel bag from the hall closet and filled it with a few of the rawhide bones lying on the floor, and several dog toys. She added a bag full of dog food and a water bowl.

"I have a refrigerator full of food," Paige said. "Can you ask the police chief about having somebody remove the food and donate it somewhere?"

"We can do that."

Paige went to a sideboard that was filled with framed photos. She paused and slowly turned to face him with panic in her eyes. "One of the photos is missing."

Dread gripped his gut. "Which one?"

"A picture of me and Kenny at Christmas."

Lucas didn't want to tell her that Colin had undoubtedly taken the photo so he would be sure to recognize Kenny. The need to get mother and son as far from Florida as possible had him saying in a sharper tone than he intended, "We're done here."

Paige grabbed two photos and stuck them into the duffel bag with Aslan's supplies. Lucas was surprised when she didn't hand him that one as well. It had to be heavy considering she had a full bag of dog food in it. When they reached the front stoop, he took the strap off her shoulder.

"I've got it," she said, hanging on to the bag.

"Go collect your son and the dog," Lucas told her.

For a moment, he thought she'd argue. After a heartbeat, she gave a quick nod, released the bag and hurried to where McIntosh pushed Kenny on the swing and Aslan lay nearby in the grass. Paige hustled the child and dog to the SUV.

McIntosh came to Lucas and relieved him of two of the bags. "She travels light," McIntosh said. "My wife would have at least three times this much stuff."

Lucas shrugged. "Maybe she realizes time is of the essence. We need to get to the airport."

"Roger that," McIntosh hustled to the back of the SUV and opened the back doors where they stowed the bags.

The drive from the neighborhood where Paige lived to the airport was slow going because of the early morning commuters.

Instead of going to the commercial terminals, McIntosh exited toward the private charter airport. The JPATS plane, part of the marshal's justice prison and alien transport system, hadn't arrived yet, so they were going to have to wait. Which didn't sit well with Lucas. He didn't like the delay.

McIntosh brought the SUV to a halt in front of the terminal. "I'll go in and see how soon your plane will land."

Lucas nodded. Keeping his head on a swivel, he stayed alert to any threats. Movement to the right caught his attention. His heart thumped against his chest. Colin Richter, aka The Beast, stepped out from behind a fuel truck. There was no mistaking the shocking white hair. In his hands, he held an automatic rifle. Two more men stepped out to flank him.

"Get down!" Lucas yelled as gunfire erupted. The sound of bullets pinging into the SUV shuddered through Lucas.

Kenny's screams filled the interior of the vehicle along with Aslan's frantic barking. Paige grabbed her son and the dog by the collar and pushed them to the floorboard, covering her son with her body.

Lucas scrambled across the middle console into the driver's seat. Thankfully, McIntosh had left the keys in the ignition. Lucas fired up the engine and threw the SUV into Reverse and stepped on the gas.

Taking fire, the vehicle jolted backward, away from the terminal and through the gate, then out to the road where he did a one-eighty turn, popped the gear into Drive and sped away.

A dark Charger came out of the gates of the private airport and chased after them. Lucas needed to lose them. Fast. He could shake them on the freeway.

Aslan quieted. Though Lucas could hear Kenny's soft sobs and his gut clenched. This shouldn't have happened.

Paige popped up and climbed over the console into the front passenger seat. She buckled her seat belt. "Take a right at the next intersection."

"What?"

She put a hand on his arm. "Trust me. I know this area. I know how we can lose them."

Now was not the time to appreciate the irony of her asking him to trust her after he'd asked her to trust him. Since he didn't know the area and was flying blind, he decided to take the chance. At the last second, he took a right and headed down a two-lane street.

"At the roundabout take the third exit," she instructed.

Behind them, the Charger made the turn amid honking horns and screeching tires.

He went around the roundabout and took the third exit, cutting off a truck, and headed down another two-lane road.

"Get ready to take the next left," Paige said.

He saw the road seconds before he gave the wheel a hard yank, going left and turning down a shaded lane overgrown with shrubbery.

"Another left," she urged.

From the back, Aslan gave a plaintive whine. Paige twisted in her seat. "Hang in there, sweetie."

Lucas hooked another left. They entered a park, passing picnic tables and sand pits for volleyball.

"Now right!"

He did as she instructed. The paved road gave way to a dirt maintenance road. They bounced along for several minutes until they came to a paved street that T'd. He glanced in the rearview mirror. The Charger was nowhere to be seen.

"Go right, again," she said.

They drove for several moments without any sign of the Charger behind them.

"Another left," Paige said.

Aslan's whining grew more insistent.

He recognized the street. They were back at her house. "What are we doing here?"

"I need to give Kenny his medication. Hurry. He's having a seizure."

Not liking the sound of that, he glanced at her. "What's wrong?"

"Pull into the driveway around back," she said.

Before he had the engine turned off, Paige had jumped out of the front passenger seat and was at the back passenger door helping Kenny and Aslan out. The boy's body jerked uncontrollably. His eyes were glassy, and his breathing labored. She hugged her son close and hustled him to the grass where she laid him down and dug out a pill bottle from her oversized purse. She stuffed a pill into his mouth and held him, speaking soothing words and rubbing his arms. Aslan paced as they waited for the medication to take effect.

"What's happening?" Lucas asked, concern for the kid arcing through him.

"Epilepsy," she said, her voice quaking. "The stress of being shot at triggered a seizure."

"Should we take him to the hospital?" Lucas only had a cursory knowledge of the disorder.

"No. He just needs a moment." She dug into her purse and brought out a garage opener and a set of keys. She held out both to him. "We can take the minivan. We can't very well ride around in that bullet-riddled contraption."

In agreement with her assessment, he took the items and pressed the button on the garage opener. The rolling door lifted, revealing a silver minivan and another car covered with a weathered tarp.

He climbed into the minivan, surprised by how clean the interior was. His sisters' vehicles were messy with their kids' food and toys. The engine roared to life and he backed out past the SUV to park so he could move the SUV into the empty spot in the garage.

He transferred luggage from the back of the SUV into the back of the minivan as she loaded up Kenny and Aslan. Kenny's breathing was easier, and he seemed more focused.

"We'll head back to the airport," he told her.

"Won't they be waiting again? They'd expect us to go back," she said.

She was right. He pulled out his cell phone and called his current boss. He explained the situation.

"Change out those license plates at the first opportunity," Gavin said.

"Will do, sir. It would be best if we don't have a police presence to advertise that we're on the move."

"Agreed. Keep me posted. If you get into any trouble again, don't hesitate to ask for backup."

"Yes, sir." He hung up and pointed to the spot next to the SUV. "What's under the tarp?"

"A Porsche 911," she said. "It doesn't run."

There was a story there, but it wasn't important. "Does it have plates?"

"It does."

He pulled the tarp off to reveal a green sports car in fairly good condition. He quickly switched out the plates from the Porsche with the plates on the minivan.

He climbed into the minivan's driver's seat and started the engine but hesitated. The ambush at the airport had not been random. Colin had known they'd be there. He'd been waiting. Could he have bugged the house? But Lucas couldn't remember mentioning the plan while inside. If they'd been tracking Paige's phone, Colin wouldn't have already been there.

Unease slithered down Lucas's spine. Who had tipped Colin off to their plan of taking the JPATS plane?

The question nagged at him as he drove away from Paige's house.

"We should take the Gulf Coast Highway," she said from the back seat. She held her son in his arms. "It will take longer but it's less obvious."

"Good thinking." He appreciated her logical mind. She

gave him directions to the highway running up the coast of Florida.

Lucas had to force himself to relax his grip on the steering wheel. This assignment wasn't going as he'd planned. He'd expected to get Paige and her son on the plane and land in San Antonio by the end of the day. He would be fortunate if they made San Antonio by tomorrow. And only if he could drive all night. But with a kid and a dog in tow, he wasn't sure that would be possible. Didn't matter. He was in this for the long haul and would do what it took to keep them all safe.

Paige held Kenny in her arms, soothing his stress. It broke her heart to see him have a seizure. She was thankful for the medication that controlled it. And for Aslan sounding the alarm. She lifted up a silent prayer. *Lord, we need You.*

"Breathe." She stroked Kenny's cheek. Aslan lay with his snout on Kenny's belly. Kenny calmed as Lucas drove them along the highway, taking them out of Fort Meyers and headed for the coastline.

Lucas's cell phone rang. The noise jolted through Paige.

"Cavendish," Lucas said. "I've got you on speaker."

"Where are you?" Special Agent McIntosh's disgruntled voice filled the interior of the minivan. "What happened?"

"We were ambushed. While you are inside." Lucas's voice was hard, his anger unmistakable.

"I was gone ten minutes, max," McIntosh stated, clearly also upset. "I heard the gunfire, but by the time I got out there, you were gone."

"Didn't last long," Lucas said.

Only because Lucas had reacted quickly. The man had saved their lives. Gratitude filled her.

"Where are you now? You need to come get me," McIntosh insisted.

"No can do. I have the witness and her son in protective custody. We are headed to our destination."

"You're going to drive all the way to San Antonio?" Mc-Intosh's voice held derision. "Keep me apprised of your location," McIntosh said. "You can't lose our witness."

McIntosh clicked off.

Paige hated being vulnerable, at the mercy of other people. Losing her husband five years ago had made her keenly aware that she could only rely on herself. "So, what is the plan?"

"Check your smartphone to see where the nearest rest stop is. I want to call my boss. But I'd like to do it stationary."

In other words, he wanted privacy. Happy to have a task, she pulled out her cell phone from the side pocket of her satchel-style purse and opened the map app to give him instructions to the nearest rest stop. Twenty minutes later, he took the exit she indicated and parked beneath the shade of a tree at the far end of the rest stop parking lot.

"We leave in five minutes."

Paige was sure Lucas had no idea that five minutes wouldn't be hardly enough. But she didn't argue with him. She leashed up Aslan and hustled her blessedly recovered son and Aslan out of the minivan. After a stop at the restroom, she led them to the grassy area to let Aslan sniff around.

She could see Lucas talking on his phone, his free hand gesturing in the air. He seemed upset. She was upset, too. He'd been assigned to protect her and yet that ghastly killer had almost managed to take her out. And her son. A shudder worked its way down her spine.

She eyed a big rig pulling into the parking lot. With the marshal focused on his phone call, Paige debated asking the truck driver for a ride. She, Kenny and Aslan could make their way to Germany. Surely the man after them wouldn't follow them to Europe, would he? Her only hope was to trust God would keep them safe from the assassin targeting them.

THREE

"Not a smart move," Lucas said in her ear.

Startled, Paige whirled around to face him. He moved quietly for such a big man. His cowboy hat shielded his eyes but she could feel his intent gaze like a laser pointer.

Aslan obviously considered him friendly because the dog hadn't given any indication of Lucas joining them.

"What are you talking about?" she hedged. There was no way the man could know what she'd been thinking. He wasn't that good. Was he?

Lucas swirled his finger in front of her. "Don't think you can fool me. I can see your brain is strategizing. You were thinking about ditching me. That would be a mistake." He thumped a finger against his chest. "I am your best option for delivering you and your son into WITSEC and making you disappear."

The chastisement stung. She didn't want to disappear. She wanted her life to go back to normal. But how could it?

He took Aslan's leash from her hand and urged her and Kenny back to the minivan. Soon they were back on the road. They hummed along for a long time with the radio playing softly and Kenny playing a game on Paige's smartphone. Aslan sat with his snout out the crack of the back passenger window. Paige scrunched up a jacket and leaned against the door, trying to rest, but calmness proved elusive, especially when Lucas began changing lanes multiple times and increasing the speed they were traveling at. From her place in the back seat, she could see him consistently checking the rearview and side mirrors.

A sense of déjà vu had Paige's heart thumping in her chest. She sat up. "What is it?"

"We have a tail."

She jerked around to stare out the back window, searching the cars and trucks behind them. The dark blue Charger cut through the traffic. The same car that had chased after them from the airport. Oh, no. *Please, Lord.* "How?"

"Throw your phone out the window," he instructed in a tight voice.

Her phone. "What?"

"They have to be tracking one of our phones," he said. "Do it."

He rolled down the back passenger window. Warm air swirled through the interior cab of the minivan.

"Kenny, I need the phone."

"Mom! I'm not done."

"Sorry, sweetie." She pried the device from his fingers and held it for a moment, mourning the loss of all the contacts and photos on it. Thankfully, most of the photos would be in the cloud. On a breath, she tossed the phone out the window and watched it bounce on the pavement before being crushed under the wheels of a semitruck.

Lucas did the same with his phone, surprising her.

Now they had no way to communicate with the outside world.

He crossed three lanes of traffic and took the next exit.

Kenny let out a whoop. "Faster!"

Horns blared behind them. The Charger didn't make the exit.

Lucas drove on the surface streets for twenty minutes

before pulling into the parking lot of a big-box store that required a membership to enter. She could only guess he was making sure the Charger hadn't found them again.

"I need to find a store that sells maps."

"As in a paper map? I don't think they exist anymore. Or at least would be hard to find."

"You're probably right. I'll have to buy a smart device." He parked and cut the engine.

"I don't have a membership to this store," she said.

"I do." He flashed her a grin.

She sucked in a breath at the way the harsh lines of his face transformed and softened. He really was handsome. Kind, too. She tore her gaze away and busied herself by hooking the leash to Aslan's therapy vest. She and Kenny joined Lucas outside the minivan. He placed one hand on her low back, his palm creating a hot spot beneath her shirt, while he took Kenny's hand in his other one.

The sight of her son so trustingly holding on to the cowboy had her heart sighing with a mix of sadness for the lack of a male in their lives and a jolt of delight to know her son wasn't afraid of Lucas.

At the entrance to the box store, Lucas showed his membership card, and they walked in. The large warehouse-style store was muggy from the afternoon heat but fans overhead whirled, circulating the air around them. Lucas led them to the electronics department and choose a tablet with Wi-Fi capabilities. In the clothing section, he grabbed a change of clothes. She hadn't considered he wasn't prepared for an overnight trip.

"We should get some snacks for the road," he said. "What kind of munchies do you two like?"

Kenny perked up. "Rice Krispies Treats."

"Trail mix," Paige said.

"Let's get both," Lucas said with a wink and steered them

to the area where large boxes of snacks waited. After making their selection, Paige moved to the rows of books and selected two that Kenny could read himself and one she could read to him.

At the checkout counter, Lucas took out his wallet to pay.

"I can do it," she said quickly, unwilling to have him eat the cost of supplies.

He waved her off. "I've got this." He peeled off several hundred-dollar bills and paid for their purchases.

As they stepped away from the cashier, she said, "Do you always carry that much money around?"

She didn't think anybody did that these days. She hadn't had more than a few dollars in her wallet at any given time for years now, but she had a stash of credit cards. Most of which had balances.

"I try to be ready for any contingency," Lucas said. "Credit cards can be traced. I don't want anyone to know where we've been."

Made sense and she appreciated his caution.

Kenny tugged on Paige's arm. "Can we get a hot dog?"

Before Paige could answer, Lucas said, "I could use one. What about you, Mom?"

She laughed. "Yes. A hot dog sounds divine."

They grabbed hot dogs and bottles of water and sat at a table to eat. Paige noticed that Lucas sat facing the entrance. He seemed to constantly scan the shoppers while he ate. His alertness alternated between making her nervous and reassuring her. He would see a threat coming, but was he really expecting one?

When they were finished eating, they left the store and climbed back into the minivan and she sighed with relief.

Their next stop was a convenience store where Lucas purchased two burner phones.

She kept Kenny busy with the books while Lucas set up

both of the phones. He handed her one. She tossed it into her satchel. Lucas called his boss. She heard his side of the conversation as he explained what they were doing. Then he called another man named James, basically repeating the information.

Curiosity burned in her gut. When he hung up, she asked, "Who did you call?"

"The marshal and my former task force leader," he explained. "I'm going to top off the gas. Then we'll be on our way."

Two hours later, Kenny finally fell asleep. She made a pillow out of jackets for him to lean against the door. Aslan lay on the floorboard, using the center hump to rest his head.

Paige climbed into the front passenger seat and buckled in.

"How is he?" Lucas asked.

"Okay. He's asleep. The seizure medication causes drowsiness," she replied.

She noticed the setting sun glinting on the gulf waters on the left side of the road. Twenty-four hours ago, her life was settled. She'd had a good job, worked for a man she respected and her son was happy. Now, her boss was dead and she and Kenny were being hunted by an assassin. "Lack of sleep can trigger a seizure."

"How long have the seizures been happening?"

"They started when he was three," she said. "He was diagnosed with epilepsy. The doctor couldn't say for sure if it was brought on by a fever or if he inherited it from his father. It doesn't run in my side of the family."

"That must've been scary."

"You have no idea," she replied and adjusted the air vents. "Those days were horrific. His first seizure—I thought I was going to lose him." Her heart rate ticked up at the memory.

"Speaking of his father, how did he die?"

Her stomach twisted at the inevitability of this question. People asked, and she understood the curiosity, but it didn't make answering any easier. "Car accident a year after Kenny was born." She shook her head. "Paul liked to drive fast. He was reckless at times. He sold high-end cars and took one out for a drive one day and wrapped it around a tree."

Lucas winced. "Must be rough raising a child on your own."

She met his gaze and wanted to lean into the warmth there but forced herself to pull back. She couldn't open her heart again, especially not to a man who was willing to risk his life for his job.

"My mom and dad helped out a lot at first. But my mom fell ill." A wave of sadness crashed over her. "My dad's focus shifted to taking care of her as it should've. When Mom passed, he couldn't take living in Florida anymore. He returned to Germany where he'd grown up."

"Munich."

"Yes." She wasn't surprised he'd remembered her mentioning the city. "Dad's going to be distraught when he hears about this."

For a moment, Lucas fell quiet. Her heart ached for the pain this situation would cause her father.

"You can't tell him." Lucas's soft voice buffeted her. "You must be aware that once you and Kenny are in witness protection, you can have no contact with your former life."

Her teeth clamped together. She did know. Hard not to when working for a federal prosecutor. But this was her life. "That's not acceptable. He doesn't live in this country. My dad knowing where we are wouldn't jeopardize our safety."

"Are you willing to stake your son's life on it?"

His question tore at her, making her want to howl with rage at the injustice of being in this horrible situation.

Lucas reached across and placed his hand on hers. "It's the way it has to be to keep you and Kenny safe."

She stared at his hand, big and capable. Warmth seeped into her skin. But there was no comfort there. She couldn't allow herself to fall victim to this man's charm. She was a job to him, and she wasn't looking to have her heart broken again. She slipped her hand out from beneath his. "I'll be safe when you have that maniac behind bars."

"You won't be safe until we know who hired him and why you are in danger. Even though you didn't see the woman who was in the office with Colin, she can't be sure you didn't see her. From the sound of it, she was the one calling the shots. I doubt she'll stop until you're eliminated."

Paige's stomach curdled. "There has to be a way for me to let my father know what's happening. I can't just disappear off the face of the earth. If I don't call him on Sunday at the appointed time— he'll move Heaven and earth to find me."

Lucas sighed. "Once we get everything in place, we'll figure out a way to get him a message. Even if I have to go there and tell him myself."

She stared at his handsome profile with her heart in her throat. "You would do that?"

"You're my witness. You're my responsibility."

Right. This was part of his job. "Given your history with the killer, I'm surprised you're not out there hunting him down."

"No more surprised than me." His voice held an edge of frustration. "I do want Colin out of the picture."

"Colin." An image of the man rose in her mind. Pale and scary. "Such an ordinary name for such a strange man."

"I call him The Beast."

"Well, it fits. I wonder if the woman I heard in Donald's office has tamed him?"

"I don't think Colin can be tamed. He likes killing too much."

Paige shuddered. "What's the story between you two?"

Lucas's hands gripped and then re-gripped the steering wheel. He was silent for a long moment. Dusk had descended without her noticing, creating shadows inside the minivan. Paige's stomach grumbled. It had been hours since they'd eaten.

"I was part of the task force out of Miami," Lucas said. "Our mission was to bring down Adam Wayne, a notorious arms dealer."

Paige gave a small gasp. "That's the case Donald was working on." She gave a small laugh devoid of any humor. "I guess the trial won't start now."

"No. A new prosecutor will be assigned to the case. Obviously. Unfortunately, the case files are missing."

"That's what Agent McIntosh told me. He also said there was some sort of corruption in the data from the cloud. I didn't know that could happen... But you helped bring down Adam Wayne?"

"Yes, I did. Eighteen months of my life were given to the mission. Along with a stellar group from ATF, DEA, NSA, DHS and NCIS."

"A regular alphabet soup."

He snorted a laugh, then grew serious, the tension in his strong jaw plain. "But now my former task force leader tells me the charges against Wayne could be dropped."

"I know the case inside and out," Paige said. "I could try to re-create what I remember."

"I doubt that would hold up in court," he said. "We'll have to start over. Build the case from scratch. Reinterview witnesses, collect new evidence."

"Unless you capture that woman and The Beast, correct? They could be the key to keeping Wayne behind bars."

"Correct."

For a long moment, Paige thought about how everything would change if they could capture these people. It would be the only way for her to have her life back. What if the US Marshals used her as bait to lure the man in?

She instinctively turned to check on her son, sleeping peacefully in the back seat. She couldn't do anything that would put Kenny in jeopardy.

Or leave him without a mother.

Aslan's hot breath fanned across Lucas's cheek. The dog had his paws up on the middle console.

"We need to stop soon," Paige said. "Aslan needs out."

"Mommy, I need to use the potty," Kenny said from the back seat.

Night had fallen hours ago. Lucas was sure they were all hungry, tired and needed the facilities. He hated to stop, but there was no avoiding it. "Check for the nearest motel."

Moments later, she was giving him directions from the tablet he'd bought. They left the highway and entered the town of Panacea and pulled into the parking lot of a one story motel. The lobby was flanked by wings of rooms with rows of blue doors marked with brass numbers.

He parked the minivan right in front of the entrance to the lobby and turned off the engine. Light from the portico spilled into the van.

"Sit tight," he said. "Honk if you need me."

"I think we'll be okay," Paige assured him. "Make sure they're dog friendly."

Confident his badge would ensure the place accepted Aslan, Lucas got out and locked the van behind him. He paused, assessing the surroundings. Light traffic on the two-lane road. A diner not far away where they could get food. A grassy area for the dog. He went inside and rented two rooms, paying cash.

"I secured adjoining rooms," he told Paige when he returned to the minivan and drove the short distance to the last two rooms on the motel's right wing. They unpacked the van and hustled inside.

"I saw a diner as we were driving in," Paige said. "After we freshen up, can we eat?"

"Good idea. I think we all could use some fuel."

"Yes, the trail mix just isn't cutting it," she said with a tired smile. Dark circles beneath her pretty eyes gave testament to the ordeal she'd suffered. He could only imagine the toll the stress of the situation was taking on her.

"I'll order and have dinner delivered," he said. "What'll you have?"

"A house salad for me, ranch dressing's fine. Chicken tenders and fries for Kenny," she said.

Retreating to his room, he made the order, getting himself a hamburger.

He quickly showered and changed into the fresh jeans and T-shirt he'd bought. Feeling human again, he was ready for the food when it arrived. He paid the kid and then knocked on the adjoining door to Paige and Kenny's room.

The door opened. Paige had also changed into fresh clothes. Soft-looking lounge pants and a matching green zip-up top made her look younger than he knew her to be.

He held up the food bag. She stepped aside and he entered. Kenny sat at a small table that had only two chairs. Lucas set out their meal on the tabletop.

"You two eat at the table," Paige insisted as she took her salad and sat on the edge of the bed.

Taking a seat across from Kenny, Lucas dug into his hamburger.

"Do you know which planet is closest to the sun?" Lucas asked after he'd finished his food.

Paige and Kenny looked at each other.

"No, which planet is closest to the sun?" Paige asked.

"Mercury," Lucas said.

"Okay," Paige said. "Didn't know that."

To Kenny, Lucas said, "How many dwarfs are there?"

"Seven," Kenny replied around a mouthful of fries.

"Can you name them?" Lucas asked.

"Can you?" Paige asked.

"Sleepy, Dopey, Happy, Crabby—"

"Nooo," Kenny groaned. "Not Crabby, Grumpy."

"Right." Lucas shared a smile with Paige and held her gaze, the clear blue of her eyes could chase away the storm brewing outside.

Attraction arced and his blood warmed. Her nearness made his senses hyperaware. The scent of the motel's shampoo smelled different on her, fresher, and made him think of a springtime meadow. She made him feel alive, less alone.

Her strawberry blond hair hung loose over her shoulders. He itched to test the texture. Would the strands be as silky as they appeared?

Giving himself a mental head slap for noticing, he glanced away. He needed to focus, not be admiring his protectee.

Abruptly, Paige stood and cleaned up the remains of their meal. "Kenny needs a bath." She handed Lucas Aslan's leash. "Would you mind taking him out?"

"Not at all." Glad for the distraction and the distance, he and the dog headed outside, locking the door behind him. He stuffed the room key in his pocket. Aslan pulled Lucas to the patch of grass. "Okay, hold your horses." He let the dog off leash to run around.

His cell phone rang. Tension rippled through him. Only

his boss had the number for the new phone. Lucas didn't recognize the number on the screen. He pressed the answer button. "Yes."

"What are you doing?" McIntosh's irate voice came over the line. "You can't keep me out of the loop."

Lucas tightened his hold on the phone. "How did you get this number?"

"My boss is breathing down my neck," McIntosh stated. "He had words with the Marshals Service and Homeland Security. This is such a mess. What are you doing with the witness? This case is imploding. Have you watched the news? We're going to lose our jobs."

"Whoa, slow down," Lucas said. "The witness is safe. We're off-the-grid. You shouldn't be calling me."

McIntosh harumphed. "Adam Wayne is going to walk. The case has fallen apart."

Anger twisted in Lucas's gut. "Not if Richter is caught. We have to flip him."

"We had a sighting around Tampa but that didn't pan out."

"You focus on finding him. Let me do my job. I'll get the witness to safety."

"How do we know she's not working with Wayne? Or Colin, for that matter."

"She's not. Colin tried to kill her."

"To tie up a loose end," McIntosh said grimly before hanging up.

Lucas put the phone in his back pocket, his mind racing. If the case against Wayne fell apart, the man would go back to supplying illegal firearms to gangs and criminals. Sometimes catching the bad guys was like playing Whac-A-Mole.

Frustrated, he whistled for the dog. Aslan came running and they headed back inside the motel.

The door between the two rooms was ajar. Aslan nudged

it open and slipped through, disappearing into Paige and Kenny's room. Lucas turned on the TV and scrolled until he found a news report.

"After the brutal murder of federal prosecutor Donald Lessing, the defense attorney for Adam Wayne is calling for the dismissal of all charges brought against the man accused of arms dealing," the news anchor said.

Lucas shook his head with disgust. How could anyone think it was a good idea to let criminals go free?

The image on the screen shifted from the news anchor to a press conference where a smartly dressed brunette stood beside the weaselly Adam Wayne. Adam's bald head shone in the bright fluorescent lights of the courthouse. "My client's rights have been violated. He has been held without bail on charges that are a fabrication by law enforcement."

Lucas's hands curled into fists. He wanted to throw something at the TV. Fabrications. They had solid proof that the man was selling illegal weapons throughout the Southwest. McIntosh's accusation stirred up doubts. Could Paige be working for Adam Wayne?

A gasp from behind Lucas had him spinning to face Paige. Her gaze was transfixed on the TV. "I recognize that voice."

FOUR

Paige stared at the sophisticated brunette speaking on the television screen. That voice. It was her. The woman who had been behind the door in Donald's office. The woman who had told the assassin to kill her.

Shock waves ricocheted through Paige's system. Ripples cascaded across her skin like a pebble skipping through the water. How could this be? How could someone like this well-spoken, well-dressed woman be a criminal?

"Paige, you know her?"

Lucas's voice tore her gaze away from the television screen to meet his. The brown warmth in his eyes anchored her, calming her. Why did he have that effect on her? His hands caressed her biceps. She hadn't even realized he'd moved to touch her. What was it about this man that made her feel safe? She wasn't safe. And she couldn't allow herself to rely on him when he would leave her just like every other person she'd ever loved. Except for her son. And even then, there would be a day when he'd go out into the world to make a life for himself apart from her. She didn't want to think that far ahead.

Best to keep an emotional and physical distance from the handsome cowboy and worry about the present situation.

She stepped back, out of his reach, and wrapped her arms around her middle. "Who is that woman?"

"Eliza Mendez. The defense attorney for the rich, the famous and the criminal."

"Really?" The woman responsible for Donald's death was part of the legal system. Outrage at the irony that the lawyer would break the law heated her blood. "And the man standing next to her is Adam Wayne."

"Yes." Lucas's hard-edged voice betrayed his anger. "The bag of trash arms dealer."

Paige swallowed back the bile rising up to burn her throat. What a twisted web she'd found herself in. "That woman is working for him?"

"Apparently, she's trying to get him set free."

The breath left Paige's lungs. It took a second before she could speak. "She's the one," her voice trembled. "She ordered Donald to be killed. She wants me dead." The words tasted bitter on her tongue.

Lucas turned to stare at the television, where Eliza continued to extol the virtues of her client, then back at Paige. "Are you sure?"

"Yes." A shudder ripped through her but she refused to give any room to the fear clamoring at the edges of her mind.

Stepping closer but not touching her, Lucas held her gaze. "No doubts?"

"None."

"You have to be one hundred percent sure," he insisted. "If we accuse her and we're wrong…this could go very badly for both of us."

Why wouldn't he believe her? "I will never forget that woman's voice. It's her."

Lucas remained silent. The urge to squirm, to flinch, under his intense regard itched like a wet wool sweater. But she held his gaze. She would not let him, or anyone, dissuade her from what she knew to be true.

Finally, he gave a sharp nod. "Okay, then. I need to make some phone calls."

Swift relief nearly had her knees buckling. "What should I do?"

Already turning away, he said, "Get some rest."

Like that was going to happen. The television screen switched to a weather map showing an incoming storm hitting the Gulf of Mexico. Paige didn't like the looks of the swirls. The high winds and rains would hit landfall sometime tonight. It would make driving difficult.

Another thought occurred to her as Lucas picked up his phone. "Are you sure you should tell people now? Shouldn't you wait until we reach San Antonio?"

He shook his head. "If I wait, there's a very good chance Wayne will be let out of jail by then. I can't take that risk."

A simmering anger burned low in her gut. "So, keeping him in jail is more important than protecting me and Kenny?"

Pain marched across Lucas's face but then his eyes hardened and his jaw firmed. "Equally as important. You're going to have to trust that I will keep you and your son safe. That is my job. I won't fail you." He flipped a hand at the TV. "But keeping Wayne off the streets is also part of my job."

Again, with the request to trust him. She'd trusted her husband but his need to be reckless had overridden his need to be safe for her and Kenny's sake. Then her father's grief over her mother's passing had driven him to leave them behind. Oh, she could have followed Dad, but he hadn't asked her to, which hurt.

Now, here was this stranger wanting her trust.

Yet, his loyalty was divided.

But her choices were limited.

She sent up a prayer that putting her trust in Lucas was the right call. Maybe she should have insisted the FBI take control of her safety. But Agent McIntosh had stressed that the US marshal was the one to protect her. She had to keep faith that the situation would work out well. And that God had a plan.

She returned to her room, pulling the connecting doors closed until there was only a crack between them. Kenny and Aslan lay snuggled on one of the queen-size beds.

"Mommy, will you pray with me?"

Tenderness filled her chest. "Of course, sweetie."

Sitting on the edge of the bed, she took his hand.

"Dear, God," Kenny's soft voice filled the room, "please help the cowboy keep us safe. Thank you for Aslan. And for Mommy. We love you. Amen."

Fighting back tears, Paige squeezed his hand. "Amen." She stood. "Go to sleep now."

Kenny rolled into a ball and threw an arm around Aslan's neck. The dog licked Kenny's face, eliciting a giggle.

Love expanded through Paige until she thought she might not be able to contain it. She would do whatever it took to keep her son from harm.

She stared at the door leading to the walkway outside. On impulse, she grabbed a chair from the desk, thankful it was the old-fashioned wooden type with the slats in the back. She may have to trust the lawman, but she wanted to do her part to keep them safe. She wedged the back of the chair underneath the door handle.

After getting herself ready for the night, she climbed into the bed wearing sweatpants and a T-shirt. She left her shoes on the floor, ready to be slipped on at a moment's notice. She turned off the light, throwing the room into shadowed darkness broken only by the faint glow of the outside parking lot lamps edging around the closed heavy curtain and the soft light peeking through the cracked connecting door.

Her head hit the pillow and exhaustion settled over her,

making her limbs heavy. She wanted to stay awake, to stay vigilant, but sleep was too great a lure.

Outside the motel room, the wind had picked up and buffeted against the windows. Lucas turned out the light and let the inky darkness settle over him before he moved across the room to peer around the edge of the curtain. The branches of the palm trees lining the parking lot blew in a back-and-forth pattern as if someone were holding the trunk and shaking the trees. Debris swirled in the air. The tapping of rain hitting the glass panes of the window constricted his nerves. A storm was brewing. Would they be able to outrun it?

Lucas's first order of business was a phone call to his boss, Gavin.

"Cavendish, where are you?" Gavin's voice came across the line, alert and steady. Did the man ever sleep?

"We're hunkered down in a motel off the highway." Getting to the heart of the matter, Lucas said, "Sir, the witness can identify the voice she heard in Donald Lessing's office before he was killed."

"What? Who is it?"

"Eliza Mendez, Adam Wayne's attorney was on the news this evening. Paige is positive that is the woman who gave the order to kill Donald."

"Voice testimony—"

"Is admissible."

"But tricky to prove reliable."

Lucas ran his hand through his hair. "Sir, I would like an armed escort from here to Texas."

"It's a secure man who can ask for help," Gavin said with approval. "I'll contact the state patrol along your route. We'll get you home safely."

"Thank you, sir. I'd like to leave here as soon as the sun makes an appearance."

"Text me the specifics of your location. I'll pass it on. Try to rest."

Gavin clicked off and Lucas texted the info, then made the call to James. Even though the task force had been dismantled and members dispersed to their various assignments within their own agencies and James promoted, Lucas figured the head honcho would want to know this alarming news that the defense attorney Eliza Mendez was not only representing Adam Wayne but had orchestrated the death of federal prosecutor Donald Lessing.

"Caveman," James Barlow said into the phone, his voice groggy. "This is a displeasure at this time of night."

Lucas winced. "Sorry, sir, can't be helped. Have you seen the news?"

James grunted. "Tell me."

"Adam Wayne is going to walk if we don't stop it. With the death of the federal prosecutor and the files missing…"

"A judge will have no option but to set him free while we build a new case." James finished Lucas's thought. "I am aware."

"His defense attorney was on the news tonight calling for Wayne's release."

"And?" Impatience threaded through the Homeland Security agent's voice. "Do you have something that will keep him behind bars?"

"No." Lucas's gut clenched. "However, my witness can place Eliza Mendez at the scene of Donald Lessing's murder."

A moment of silence followed that pronouncement.

"Is this credible?" James sounded more alert now.

"Yes, sir. My witness is positive."

"She saw her there?" An excited hum reverberated through the line.

"The witness heard Eliza Mendez's voice. First in Donald Lessing's office and then later when Colin Richter tried to kill the witness."

"Well, this could be something. Though courts have ruled voice recognition admissible, it's tricky to prove. The defense could say she was in a heightened state and her memory isn't reliable."

"I believe her, sir. She is credible."

"This is the paralegal who worked for Lessing, correct?"

"Yes, sir."

"And how do we know she's not working with the assassin? And isn't trying to deflect blame onto the defense attorney?"

Lucas fisted his free hand. "That's not the case, sir. My gut tells me she's telling the truth. She's on the up and up."

"Well, if your gut says so," James's voice held sarcasm. "You need to find proof. And if what you say is true, you need to double down on your protection of the witness."

Tension corkscrewed through Lucas. "I understand, sir."

"Good. We'll talk more when the sun is actually shining." James hung up.

Lucas tucked his phone into the breast pocket of his shirt.

Fatigue pulled at the muscles in his neck and shoulders. His alert gaze kept watch outside the window. Was that a shadow moving across the lot?

His heart pounded in his chest. He moved to the other side of the window to view from a different angle. Better safe than sorry. He retrieved his room key and secured his service weapon at his side. He eased out of the motel room door. The shadow he'd seen may have been nothing more than an animal or another guest going to their room. But being overly cautious was never wrong. A perimeter sweep was in order.

* * *

Paige jerked awake. She lay still for a moment, assessing, listening. The motel room was quiet. She couldn't quite determine the time of night. She sat up and reached for her phone. A noise near the exterior door drew her attention and she froze.

Her gaze jumped to the other bed. She saw Kenny's silhouette but not Aslan's.

She grimaced. The dog sat in front of the exit and obviously needed out. With a sigh, she pushed back the covers, slipped her feet over the side of the bed, and found her shoes. She walked softly to the desk where she'd left the leash. Then she hesitated.

Was it safe to go outside?

She had Aslan. Without a doubt, he would protect her. And normally, she wouldn't think twice about stepping out the door into the dark night.

But her world had been turned upside down. An assassin was after her. A powerful woman wanted her dead.

Safe was a moving target.

Plus, the wrath she would incur if she stepped outside without letting the marshal know had her nerves twitching.

With a wry twist of her lips, she set the leash back down and headed to the connecting doors. She pulled open the door on her and Kenny's side of the room. It was dark through the crack on Lucas's side of the room. Careful not to wake Kenny, she softly tapped a fingernail against the door. Then slowly pushed it open.

She waited, listening for a rustling of the covers or his strong voice but there was only silence. Hesitantly, she stepped into Lucas's room.

The room wasn't as dark as she'd first thought. The blackout draperies had been pushed aside leaving only the sheer white curtains covering the window and allowing light from outside to spill into the room. Both beds were made. His cowboy hat sat on the desk. Her gaze swung to the restroom. The door was open and the room dark.

Panic revved through her blood. He was gone. He'd left her and Kenny alone.

She backpedaled toward the connecting door when the air swirled around her with movement and a hand clamped on her arm. She let out a startled yelp.

"You needed something?" Lucas's soft voice reached out to her like a caress.

She shivered. "Where were you?"

"Here." His hand softened on her arm, and his thumb rubbed against her skin, creating a hot spot that sent warmth spreading up her arm to her cheeks. "What do you need?"

She swallowed past the constriction in her throat. "Aslan needs to go out."

"I'll take him." Gripping her gently by the elbow, he ushered her back into her room. He released her so that she could leash Aslan and then she handed him the lead.

"Keep that door locked," he ordered.

Lucas led Aslan through the connecting doors back to his room. She moved to the window and pushed the curtain aside to watch as the pair ambled away from the motel across the parking lot through the rain and wind to the patch of grass surrounded by bushes.

"Unhook him," she muttered under her breath. Tethered, Aslan would think he needed to be working.

Aslan stood still, waiting. Lucas squatted down and seemed to be talking to him. Then he unhooked the leash. Paige let out a relieved breath. The dog gave him a swipe with his tongue before he loped away, sniffing the ground until he found a spot to do his business.

Aslan trotted back to Lucas and then turned in a circle,

his tail high and his ears back. Clear signs that something was wrong.

Paige's heart thumped painfully against her ribs. Lucas quickly clipped the leash back onto Aslan's collar and tugged him back toward the motel, while keeping his free hand on his sidearm.

The headlights of a car flicked on and shone through the bushes. The car sped away in a squeal of tires on wet pavement.

Lucas and Aslan jogged back to the motel.

Paige hurried to Lucas's room. As soon as he entered and locked the door behind him, she asked, "What happened?"

"I'm not sure," he said, shaking the water out of his hair. "But we should leave."

The grimness of his tone sent dread rippling down her back. Not about to argue, she hurried back to her room and packed up the few belongings she'd taken out.

Lucas walked into the room. "I'll get the bags. You get your son."

Transferring a sleeping Kenny to the back seat of the minivan during a storm took every ounce of Paige's resilience. She strapped him in and leaned him against a confiscated pillow from the motel.

She promised silently that she would send the motel money to make up for the loss of the pillow.

They were on the road within minutes of the van doors shutting. Wind and rain slashed through the night sky. The windshield wipers couldn't seem to keep up.

"Where are we headed?" she asked Lucas.

"To the next town. Then I'll call my bosses."

"Do you really think someone found us?" He set his phone on the console with the navigation system giving directions.

"I'm not about to take any chances."

She kept an eye on the side-view mirror. But there was nobody else crazy enough to be out in the storm. The minivan drifted on the water sloshing over the road. Paige gripped the door handle and prayed for safety. Finally, the next small town came into view. Instead of going to a hotel, Lucas drove directly to the police station.

He parked in the lot, turned off the engine and faced her. "From here on out, we'll have an escort."

If he thought that was going to make her feel better, he was wrong. Having an escort would only make them more conspicuous. More of a target. Was she making a mistake trusting this man?

FIVE

After securing an escort from the Florida State Troopers to the Alabama state line and deciding with the troopers to take backroads to stay away from the more crowded highways, Lucas battled the wind blowing across the road and wanting to wrest control of the minivan away from him. Rain tapped a steady beat on all sides of the vehicle, a relentless sound he found hard to ignore.

When they reached the state line, their Florida escorts peeled off and an Alabama State Trooper cruiser took up the vigil, following behind them at a close distance while traversing the backroads of the state.

Paige had moved to the back bench seat to sit with her son. The two played the game I Spy and sang a variety of children's songs, reminding Lucas of road trips with his parents and sisters. Had his father enjoyed those days?

Dad wasn't big on outward displays of emotion or affection. At least not until he'd had grandkids. Dad and Mom doted on Lucas's oldest sister Yvette's twin girls, and his middle sister Autumn's son.

Lucas and Lily, his sister closest in age but still older by twelve months, were both unmarried, with no kids. Mom and Dad had been hinting lately that it was time for them both to remedy that situation. Lucas figured he had plenty of time. He'd let Lily be next in the family to find a spouse and bring more grandkids into the world.

Lucas admired the deep bond apparent between Paige and her son. He hoped if he ever did start a family, he would have that same sort of bond with his kid. But he wasn't ready for that type of commitment. His job required too much focus. And risk. While in the military he'd seen too many flag-draped caskets and grieving widows to ever want to put someone through that pain.

Despite the storm raging outside the vehicle and in his own heart, he found himself humming along to Paige and Kenny singing one of his nieces' favorite animated movie songs about friendship.

They stopped every few hours to let the dog and Kenny out to run around. Lucas touched base with the troopers and watched the antics of Kenny and Aslan. He never realized how much energy a six-year-old had. He admired the patience with which Paige dealt with her son and the dog.

After the last stop, Paige tucked Lucas's coat around Kenny.

"Hopefully he'll sleep," she said. "I heard you humming. A childhood favorite?"

Lucas laughed. "Two of my sisters have kids."

"Ah. That explains why you're so good with Kenny. You've had practice," she said. He could feel her gaze. "I never thought to ask. Are you married? Kids?"

"No and no."

Lucas's phone rang. He put it on speaker. "Cavendish."

"I understand from your boss that the witness can identify the voice of the woman in the office with Donald Lessing." McIntosh's voice filled the interior of the minivan.

Lucas glanced in the rearview mirror and met Paige's gaze. She arched an eyebrow.

"That's correct."

"Where are you?" McIntosh asked. "We need to get her into the nearest FBI office to listen to voice samples so we can verify that she can truly identify the woman."

Ignoring the question, Lucas addressed the issue that made his blood pressure rise. "We can do that when we get to Marshal headquarters. But she's sure the woman was Eliza Mendez."

"We're trying to establish Mendez's whereabouts the night of Donald's murder."

"You need to find the truth," Lucas insisted. "We need to keep Adam Wayne behind bars."

"Believe me, we're on it. No one wants to see Wayne freed."

"We'll talk again when we reach San Antonio."

Lucas clicked off.

Up ahead, road hazard signs blinked in the dim gray light of the storm. Road construction? In the middle of a storm?

Lucas slowed as dread gripped his gut. Though there was no way for anyone to know which route they were taking, unless somehow they'd infiltrated the Alabama State Troopers, he slowed and called the troopers.

"Cavendish here," Lucas said. "Are you aware of any road construction going on?"

"No, sir," came the reply. "I'm thinking those signs are a signal to use caution. There's an old wooden bridge up ahead."

"Makes sense," Lucas said and clicked off.

Rain and gusts of wind slammed against the side of the minivan. With an effort, he kept the vehicle in a straight line. He glanced back in the rearview mirror, past Paige's wide eyes, to the Alabama State Troopers' vehicle behind them. Through the pounding rain, he could make out the two round orbs of their headlights.

Up ahead, the bridge came into view spanning a wide creek. Water sloshed over the sides of the guardrail of the wooden bridge.

Gripping the steering wheel, he held his foot steady on the gas as they motored over the bridge and through the layer of rising creek water. The back end of the minivan fishtailed on the slick wood. Thankful, they made it to the other side just as a loud cacophony of noise shuddered through him.

"The bridge!"

At Paige's exclamation, Lucas chanced another glance in the rearview mirror. His heart jumped in his chest. The bridge had collapsed behind them, and pieces of wood and twisted metal stuck out from the water. On the other side of the creek at the entrance to the bridge, the Alabama State Troopers' vehicle halted.

Lucas brought the minivan to a stop. His phone rang. He pushed the button to answer. "Cavendish."

"This is Alabama State Trooper Lenny Corbin, this is the end of the line for us. You have fifteen miles before you reach the Louisiana border. The state troopers will pick you up again."

"I appreciate the heads-up. Stay safe," Lucas said into the phone before clicking off.

"Should we find shelter?" Paige asked.

They were surrounded by dense woods all around them. "As soon as we hit the state line and have our escorts, we'll find somewhere to ride out the rest of the storm."

He drove cautiously for another couple of miles. A service station came into view. There was a single building and one island with two gas pumps. The place looked abandoned with no lights on and no cars waiting to fill up.

"Could we see if they have a restroom?" Paige asked.

Debating with himself, he pulled the minivan in front of

the building and sat idling, staring at the darkened structure for a moment. Caution ticked along the column of his spine.

"I don't think anybody's here," Paige said as she leaned over the front console. "Maybe the restrooms are around back?"

The harsh wind and relentless rain hammered at the vehicle. "We can check."

He pressed the accelerator and drove around to the back of the building once again halting as a small dark blue four-door sedan came into view parked by the back doors. The license plate was from Florida. It stood to reason there were other travelers who might've sought shelter here. But unease raised the hairs at the nape of his neck and pimpled the skin along his arms. He sent up a quiet plea to God to give him discernment.

Would it be safe for them to venture out? Would the people here be friends or foes?

The internal alarm system didn't quit, instead his sense of foreboding only intensified. He'd learned to listen to the warnings of his gut. Lucas backed up the minivan and made a U-turn, heading them back out on the road.

"What is it?" Paige asked, climbing over the console, and settling into the passenger seat. She pulled the seat belt across herself and buckled in. "Why aren't we stopping there?"

Lucas would sound kooky, but he told her the truth, anyway. "I have a really bad feeling about that place."

She remained silent as he concentrated on putting distance between them and the gas station. Should he have stuck with the more trafficked highway rather than opting for backroads? Would Paige think she'd made a mistake trusting him to protect her and Kenny?

"Okay, then," she said. "We cross into Louisiana and then find somewhere to use the restroom."

Her acceptance of his explanation surprised and pleased him.

The storm grew heavier and more insistent. The sky darkened with the raging weather. The wipers slashed over the windshield, clearing the rainwater away with a frantic beat that couldn't seem to keep up.

A bend in the road loomed ahead.

Glancing in the rearview mirror, a dark shape took form. The car from the gas station? Or was someone else braving the storm?

Both sides of the country road they traveled dipped down into water-filled ravines that bordered deep dense woods.

"Lucas, look out!" Paige shrieked.

Swinging his gaze back to the road, his heart slammed against his rib cage. He stomped on the brakes, the front tires screeching on the wet pavement. The minivan came to a halt, inches from where the heavy rains had washed out a chunk of the road.

There was no going forward. He would have to turn the minivan around and go back. Maybe his gut had been wrong. Maybe his gut had been telling him to seek shelter at that gas station and not to move on. He'd asked God for discernment and perhaps Lucas hadn't been listening.

A car came around the bend in the road.

The dark blue sedan that had been parked behind the gas station.

Had the driver been lying in wait for them? It was too coincidental that the occupant of the car decided to leave so soon after Lucas had driven away from the only shelter for miles.

The car stopped several yards from them. A man climbed out.

There was no mistaking the ghastly snowy hair and skin of Colin Richter.

Fear jolted through Lucas. They were trapped. The road was gone in front of them, and the bridge was down behind them. He couldn't drive the minivan into the woods because of the drainage ditches on both sides of the country road. Frantic to protect his charges, he said, "We have to get out and make a run for it into the woods."

Paige let out an audible gasp. "That's him. The man who wants to kill me."

"It is. Hurry!"

"Kenny, grab your coat!" Paige unbuckled quickly and climbed back through the middle console to help her son into his jacket before shrugging into her own. She leashed up the dog and grabbed her big satchel purse where Lucas knew she kept Kenny's medicine. He jumped out and ran around to open the sliding door.

He held on to his cowboy hat as the wind tried to lift it from his head. With his free hand, he took the dog's leash from Paige. "Move."

"There's a flashlight in the glove box," Paige told him.

"Mommy, I'm scared." Kenny clung to his mother's side.

"I know, sweetie," Paige soothed him but urged him away from the vehicle.

After grabbing the flashlight and tucking it into his waist band, Lucas said, "We have a better chance if we cross to the other side of the collapsed road." Taking Kenny from Paige, he gestured. "Jump."

She hesitated, then ran and jumped across the divide.

Dropping Aslan's leash, Lucas yelled to her, "Call the dog."

"Aslan! Here, boy." Paige patted her thighs.

The dog barked but didn't move.

Lucas glanced back. Colin stalked toward them.

Taking a running jump, Lucas with Kenny in his arms, sailed over the empty space in the road where the asphalt gave way. With a leap, Aslan joined them.

Setting Kenny on his feet, Lucas pointed to the drainage ditch. "Go. Into the woods."

Slipping down the side of the open drainage ditch, they waded through knee-high brackish water and weeds to the other side. Using their hands and knees, they climbed up the embankment. Bits of debris shot up next to Lucas. A rock bounced off his cheek.

He looked over his shoulder. Colin stood on the edge of the road. His weapon, fitted with a noise suppressor, was aimed at them. Lucas maneuvered himself so that he was behind Kenny and Paige, shielding them from harm. He fired at Colin, hitting him in the arm.

Lucas urged Paige and Kenny to move faster up the last bit of the hill. "Go. Run as far and as fast as you can. Stay in the trees. I'll find you."

"Wait! What are you…?" A bullet slammed into the earth close to her head.

On a yelp, Paige wrapped an arm around her son, lifted him off his feet, and ran toward the woods. Lucas sent a thankful prayer for the wind and rain and the wound, which had caused Colin's poor aim. Lucas let go of Aslan's leash and the dog ran after his people.

Lucas flipped to his back, dug the heels of his cowboy boots into the rocks and loose dirt of the embankment and aimed his weapon. Blinking the rainwater from his eyes, he fired. A gust of wind yanked at his weapon.

Colin screeched and ducked behind the minivan.

"We end this now!" Lucas called out.

He scrambled back down the ditch, through the water and up the other side. When he reached the crest of the road, he saw Colin running with a noticeable limp back to his vehicle. Getting to his feet, Lucas fired into the sedan, taking out the front windshield. Colin jumped inside and put the car in Reverse. Lucas fired again, the bullet slamming into the front of the vehicle. Then the sedan spun in a half circle, fishtailed and sped away.

Lucas led out a primal scream. He'd failed to take out Colin Richter again.

But at least The Beast hadn't harmed Paige or Kenny.

Lucas noticed the blood trail on the pavement smeared by the pounding rain. Lucas took grim satisfaction in knowing he'd wounded the other man. That would slow him down.

Not wasting another moment, Lucas ran down into ditch, doing his best not to go face-first into the water. Then he scrambled up to the other side, the rocks and debris cutting into his hands and knees.

Tall weeds and marshy grass were bent where Paige, Kenny and Aslan had run, creating a trail for him to follow. But once he hit the trees, the trail was harder to track. He needed to find them. He needed to keep them safe.

How had Richter known what route they had been taking? Someone must have told him. Lucas vowed he'd find the truth and make whomever sold them out pay dearly.

The wind howled through the trees. The rain stung her face, pushing Paige farther into the murky depths of the Alabama woods. Kenny grew heavy in her arms, making her progress slower than she wanted. Her legs burned from the exertion. Aslan ran ahead, then circled back and again ran ahead. Were they headed for Louisiana? Should she double back and find the road?

The sound of gunfire had shuddered through her, then stopped, eliciting images of Donald, blood and death.

She had to save her son. And herself.

Was Lucas hurt? Was another person going to die? Why was she surrounded by death? Her husband, her mother and Donald. Now maybe Lucas. A sob rose but she refused to give room to the swelling grief. There would be time for that later. Her priority was getting to safety.

The underbrush of the swampy woods slapped at her legs. Water soaked through her clothing, making the material chaff against her skin. Tears and raindrops mingled to run down her face. Her breath came out on labored puffs. The musky scents of the forest filled her lungs.

Aslan paused, his tail standing up and his ears back.

Was it the assassin coming after them? Panicked, she headed for a close grouping of trees and bushes. She circled behind them, setting Kenny on the ground even as he clung to her.

"Honey, I need you to listen. I want you to squeeze in between these trees. Don't come out until I tell you."

"No, Mommy." Kenny fisted his hands in her jacket. "We have to run. That's what the cowboy said."

She pointed with a finger at the small space in between the trees. It would provide him with some coverage. "Inside. Now."

Aslan barked, a frantic sound that sent a shiver of dread over Paige's flesh. She gave Kenny a gentle push. He scrambled into the space among the trees.

"Hunker down," she told him before moving away.

She searched the ground for something to defend herself with. If she could get the drop on the assassin, get him from behind or even from the side, and hit him with a rock or a branch, she might have a fighting chance. There. A broken limb from a tree lay on the ground. She darted forward, grabbed the end of the branch and dragged it back to the shelter of the trees. She gave a sharp whistle. Aslan came running. She grabbed him by the collar. She looked him in the eye. "Stay."

She pointed the dog's snout toward her son. She wasn't sure if Aslan understood but Kenny was the priority.

Paige hunkered down with the tree limb held like a bat in her hands. It was heavy and made her arms ache, but she didn't care.

Pounding footsteps drew closer and closer. Her body tensed. Aslan gave a bark. She shot the dog a glare and noticed his tail thumping against the tree trunk. What gives?

"Paige, where are you?" Lucas's voice came at her on the wind.

She sagged momentarily with relief. Cautiously, she peered out around the grouping of trees and saw Lucas slogging toward her. His clothes were plastered to his brawny frame and his cowboy hat was pulled low over his face. He spun in a circle, looking in all directions. She didn't see anyone else other than Lucas. Did that mean he'd— She couldn't bring herself to think about what might've happened back on the road.

She dropped the branch and stepped out. "Lucas!"

He spun toward her, a mix of relief and something she didn't understand crossing his face before he sprinted to her side. He wrapped her in his arms and pushed her back behind the tree.

"Where's Kenny?"

Kenny squeezed out of the opening between the trees and wrapped his arms around Lucas's leg. "I'm here, cowboy. I'm here."

Lucas dropped to his knee and hugged the boy close.

Paige's heart thumped, then liquefied in her chest. Seeing her son engulfed in Lucas's strong arms made her ache with a longing she didn't want to examine.

Aslan moved in to swipe his tongue across Lucas's face.

The man laughed and grabbed the dog around the neck for a hug. He tipped his head back and peered at Paige from beneath the brim of his cowboy hat, his brown eyes filled with tenderness. She had no defenses against that look. Her heart thumped in her chest and an answering tenderness bloomed within her. She was too tired and scared to fight it.

With a hand, he reached for hers. She clung to him.

Seeming to gather his breath, he released Kenny and Aslan, then rose to his full height. "We need to get out of here."

"What happened? Is he—"

"I grazed him. He escaped." Lucas shook his head. "But I know Colin Richter. He'll regroup and come back stronger."

Not the pronouncement she was hoping for.

Wrapping an arm around her waist, and his other arm around Kenny's shoulders, he urged them forward, deeper into the woods.

Leaning into him, she asked, "Are you sure we're headed in the right direction? I'm a bit turned around."

"I'm praying so. The state line shouldn't be too much farther. Then we'll head to the road and find the troopers."

She wrapped her arm around his waist and gave him a squeeze.

His gaze jerked to her.

"I'm praying, too," she told him. More than ever, they needed God's guidance and protection. When would this nightmare end?

SIX

Lucas's heart still pounded way too fast in his chest. He could only thank God and the wind for thwarting Colin's aim. Though Lucas had to admit his own aim hadn't fared any better because of the storm.

Colin would've killed Lucas otherwise.

Thankfully, he was alive and had been able to find Paige and Kenny safe. As he pushed them onward, deeper into the swampy woods filled with who knew what kind of critters, he kept up a silent litany of prayers asking God for intervention.

He wanted to put as much distance as possible between them and Colin. The bridge had collapsed behind them, and the road had given way in front of them. The minivan wasn't an option.

And somewhere out there, Colin was treating his wounds and when he was done, he'd resume his hunt.

It grew darker by the second the deeper they trudged forward into the woods. He hoped they were moving parallel to the road and would eventually meet up with the Louisiana State Troopers. He saw an outcropping of trees and a boulder and led Paige and Kenny into its shelter. He dug his phone from his pocket. No bars to indicate a cell signal. Either they were too far out in the country for cell coverage or the storm had knocked out a cell tower. He sent a text to his boss anyway, explaining the situation, because at some point they would come across cell service and the text would go through.

"We have to be close to the state line by now," he told Paige. "We'll veer south. That should take us back toward the road."

"It will be dark soon," she said. "Do you think the troopers will wait for us?"

The concern had crossed his mind as well. "Let's keep moving."

Aslan nudged Kenny with his snout and whined.

Paige knelt in front of her son and held his face in her hands. "Are you feeling faint? Dizzy?"

Lucas could see that the boy's eyes were glassy. Shivers racked his small body. They were all sopping wet and cold. Was another epileptic episode coming on?

He crouched down next to Paige and put his hand on the boy's shoulder. "Kenny, we are safe. Nothing's going to get you. I promise I will keep you safe. Hang in there with us."

Kenny shifted his gaze to meet Lucas's. "I'm hungry."

"It shouldn't be too much longer." At least Lucas hoped so.

Paige leaned into Lucas to say, "It's too soon to give him preventative medicine. But if he has a seizure, I have rescue medication to give him." She patted her satchel.

Lucas lifted Kenny into his arms. "How about I carry you for a bit?"

The boy lay his head on Lucas's shoulder. Tenderness welled within his chest, a sensation Lucas was becoming familiar with when around Paige and Kenny.

Paige's smile and the affection in her eyes made him stumble.

"A root," he said to cover his reaction. He regained his balance and tightened his hold on Kenny.

Stay focused, he admonished himself.

As they continued forward, the night settled over the world and the sounds of nocturnal animals could be heard over the swoosh of the wind through the branches and the continual rain. A night owl hooted from the trees. The scents of the earth stirred by the wind and rain intensified the musty odor that conjured up images of death and decay.

He forced the dire thoughts out of his mind.

Aslan darted forward, his barking echoed through the trees.

"Do you think he'll be safe?" Paige asked.

"Dogs have good instincts. Besides, he's quick and smart."

Picking up the pace, they hurried to find the dog had broken through to a clearing where a small dark cabin stood, an inky silhouette against the trees. Aslan pranced back and forth in front of the place as if proud of himself for finding it. Lucas gave a laugh. He was proud of the dog, too. Lucas set Kenny on his feet and approached the front porch. To be sure no one was inside, Lucas gestured for Paige and Kenny to stay behind him as he knocked loudly on the wooden door.

There was no stirring from within. He tried the doorknob. Locked. He didn't want to kick the door in. Too destructive. There were other ways of entering a locked premises. He turned to Paige, gesturing with his chin toward the large satchel anchored to her shoulder. "Any chance you have a paper clip in there? Or a safety pin?"

"I do." She dropped to her knees, setting the satchel on the ground so she could rummage through the pockets. A moment later, she produced two paper clips.

"Will these do?"

"Perfect." Lucas took the two silver spirals from her hand and quickly manipulated the metal, turning one into a tension wrench while the other he used as a pick. Within minutes, he had the door unlocked and they were inside, sheltered from the storm. He relocked the door behind them.

"Let's take our shoes off," Paige said. "No need to track mud all over the place."

Admiration warmed him. Even when running for her life, she cared about how she treated others.

Ambient light from outside crept through the windows as Lucas braced a hand on the wall and tugged his cowboy boots off. His wet socks squished on the floor.

Using the flashlight he'd taken from the minivan, Lucas swept the main room. A table with four chairs sat in the corner near what could only be described as a kitchenette. A worn couch and an armchair sat facing a woodburning stove. A ladder led to a second floor. He checked the walls and found the light switch. Two standing lamps on either side of the couch came on, the soft glow making the cabin less stark.

"Let's close the curtains on the windows. We don't want to advertise that we're here."

"Are we safe?" The quake in her voice had his gut clenching. She and Kenny were holding up well under the strain of running for their lives.

He wished he could make this easier for her, for them. "We are. At first light, we'll head out."

He moved to the kitchen area and pulled the dark blue curtains together while Paige did the same to the living room windows. Some light would shine around the edges of the curtains and under the doorframe, but that was a chance they were going to have to take. He looked for a landline phone but didn't find one. He checked for a cell signal and there were still no bars.

The cabin was well-kept and stocked with stacks of bottled water and boxes of protein bars next to the compact refrigerator. There was a tiny sink and cupboards beside an apartment-sized four-burner stove-and-oven combo.

"Upstairs there might be clothes we can borrow," Paige said.

"I'll go first." He climbed up the ladder that led to a loft-style bedroom and adjoining bath. He found the light switch and soft wall sconces illuminated the space. One bed and a bedside table were the only pieces of furniture. Rain tapped against a curtainless window in the apex of the sloped roof. A single-door closet was next to the bath.

He held out a hand to Paige and helped her into the loft. She, in turn, helped Kenny. Aslan barked from the bottom of the ladder.

"Sorry, boy, you'll have to wait for us," Paige said. She peeked into the bathroom. "There's a shower and clean towels. Kenny—"

She didn't have to ask him twice. Kenny hurried to the bathroom and shut the door.

Chuckling, Lucas checked under the bed and found several watertight plastic boxes. He dragged them out. "I'm sure we can find something warm within these."

Without hesitation, Paige opened the lid and tugged out warm flannel shirts and dry socks. She shed her jacket and pulled off her soaked socks, revealing her red-painted toenails. A sharp-edged heat zinged through his blood.

"I'll give you some privacy while I gather fuel for the woodstove." He climbed down the ladder, stepped back into his boots and headed out into the storm, grateful for the cold air. He breathed in deeply and took a moment to gather his thoughts and his emotions. He admired Paige and her commitment to her son. His respect for her grew every moment they were together. And he couldn't deny the attraction arcing through him. She was beautiful, kind and caring. Courageous and determined. There was so much about her to like, to fall for.

But he couldn't allow himself to fall for her. He had a job to do. Which did not include developing feelings for his witness.

Snuggling deep into the oversized flannel shirt and long johns she'd found in the confines of the clothing tubs, Paige pulled up the warm socks over the bottom edges of the long johns. She'd showered, the warm water chasing away the chill of the storm. She'd found a closet with hangers to hang their clothes, so they'd air dry.

"What you think, Mama?" Kenny asked. He'd put a sweatshirt on that hung past his knees. He wore socks that flopped like clown shoes. But he was clean, dry and warm. A blessing for sure.

"Let me roll the sleeves up for you." She quickly rolled the sleeves practically all the way to his shoulder so that his little arms could stick out.

She helped him climb down the ladder. Lucas was still outside. She settled Kenny on the couch with a thick wool throw she'd found.

After checking the refrigerator, which was empty except for some condiments, and the cupboards containing a few canned goods, she removed three bottles of water.

She found a small bowl and opened one of the water bottles and poured some into it for Aslan. While he lapped up the water, she unscrewed a bottle and took a long drink for herself. Then she handed the rest of the bottle to Kenny, who sipped at it.

"It's important we stay hydrated," she told him.

Kenny nodded and drank deeper of the water.

Aslan raced across the little cabin to the door. Sudden apprehension grabbed ahold of Paige. Her throat tightened and her blood raced along her limbs. She moved to stand in front of Kenny seconds before the door opened. Paige's heart thumped in her chest at the now familiar sight of their cowboy protector. He carried an armload of wood. Water dripped off his cowboy hat and puddled on the floor. Their gazes met. His lips curved into a slow smile. Warmth crept up her neck and into her cheeks. She hurried to close the door behind him.

"I'll get a fire started," he murmured, moving to the woodstove.

After securing the lock, she pressed her back against the cool wood. She'd forgotten the pleasure of having a confident man around. But it was more than just a male's presence that created a deep awareness of Lucas. There was something about the marshal that elicited a sense of well-being and safety in the midst of a crisis. His calm demeanor. His surety of purpose. All very appealing and attractive traits.

She was beginning to like this man way more than she should. He wasn't there as some surrogate husband or father. He was there to protect her and Kenny from a brutal assassin. Letting herself become attached wasn't smart. She didn't want to open her heart up and risk more hurt. Eventually, they'd part ways. Him on to his next dangerous assignment, while she and Kenny returned to a nice, safe life. One without the fear of trauma.

Giving herself a mental shake, she used a roll of paper towels she'd found under the sink and sopped up the rainwater from the floor. With that task done, she opened a can of carrots. She rinsed them in the sink to wash away as much sodium as possible in order to feed them to Aslan. Once he was eating, she opened a can of ranch-style beans, along with another can of carrots and dumped both cans into a saucepan. She turned the knob on the stove, but nothing happened.

"The gas must be turned off," she said.

"You can heat food on the woodstove," Lucas told her.

A fire blazed in the belly of the black woodstove. His boots were off and were sitting in front of the stove to dry. He'd moved hers and Kenny's shoes over as well so they could catch some of the heat, too. A very thoughtful gesture. He'd placed his signature cowboy hat on the back of the armchair.

"While the food is warming, why don't you go shower and find some dry clothes?" she said. He had to be chilled and uncomfortable.

He hesitated. She figured he didn't want to leave them vulnerable to an attack. She didn't blame him. "Aslan will protect us and sound an alarm if anyone gets close."

Lucas seemed to think over her words, then he handed her his sidearm. "Keep this close."

Staring at the weapon, her pulse tripped through her veins. "I've never handled a gun."

"It's only dangerous if you squeeze the trigger." He laid the gun on a shelf out of Kenny's reach. "Hopefully, you won't need it. But it's there. Aim and pull."

"You make it sound so simple," she commented, turning her gaze away from the weapon.

"It's a tool." He grabbed the iron poker that was propped against the woodstove. "This is also a tool." He swiped the air with it like a sword. "This could do some serious damage."

She appreciated that he was giving her options of ways to protect herself. Though neither option made her feel safe. Not like he did.

He set the poker down and then disappeared up the ladder. A few moments later, she heard the shower turn on.

She busied herself warming up the food. She found bowls, spoons and a box of crackers. She set the table, the act of domesticity somehow settling her nerves. The beans and carrots were bubbling when Lucas returned wearing dry socks, sweatpants cinched at the waist and a hoodie sweatshirt.

"Dinner's ready," she called to Kenny.

They sat at the table and ate in silence for several moments. The food was warm and nourishing and tasted better than she expected.

"I didn't know I liked these," Kenny said. "Beans are good."

Paige laughed. "When we get back home we'll have to try them again."

"You've never had these kinds of beans?" Lucas said. "They were a staple in my family on summer camping trips."

"This is as close to camping as we've come." Paige told him. Somehow, the admission made her feel guilty like she'd deprived her son.

"There's plenty of time in the future to go camping," Lucas assured her. "And there's all types of camping. What we're doing right here is a sort of camping. But my sisters would say we're glamping. A more glamorous sort of camping."

"Yea," Kenny said. "We're camping."

"How many sisters do you have?"

"Three. All older. Only two are married with kids."

"Do they go camping?" Kenny asked.

"Yep. Every summer the family heads to the Texas Hill Country and one of the many lakes," he said. "There's fishing, boating and swimming. As well as roasting marshmallows over a fire and playing games."

Grateful to Lucas for keeping the conversation and the mood light, she couldn't help but wonder what it would be like to go camping with this man. The whole idea of sleeping in a tent, cooking over a fire and battling bugs hadn't ever appealed to her, but suddenly the idea of being outdoors, under the stars and having fun on a lake sounded interesting. Like maybe something she should try, as long as Lucas was part of the picture.

Mulling over the outlandish thought, she took their empty bowls to the sink where she washed them and set them aside to dry. She really needed to get a grip on her emotions. Becoming attached to Lucas wasn't a smart plan. Thinking of a future where he was a part of the equation was setting herself up for disappointment and heartache.

"You two should get some rest," Lucas said, drawing her attention. Dark circles underscored his deep brown eyes. "Take the bed upstairs."

"You need rest, too. Aslan will alert you if anyone approaches," Paige said, her voice stern. She had no doubt he intended to sit up all night, keeping watch.

Lucas arched an eyebrow. "Is that in order?"

Placing her hands on her hips, she nodded. "It is."

He dipped his chin. "Yes, ma'am."

Paige laughed and rolled her eyes. The man was certainly charming and attractive and way off-limits. She didn't need another adrenaline-junkie type of man in her life. She didn't want to go through the pain of having their world turned upside down again. Raising Kenny was her focus. She couldn't lose sight of her priorities.

She herded Kenny up the ladder. They snuggled into the bed, grateful for the thick down comforter. She heard Aslan's nails clicking against the wood floor of the cabin before he settled down. She hoped Lucas would rest. They would both need their wits about them come daylight.

The rhythmic cadence of the rain lulled her, making her eyelids heavy.

Please, Lord, let us make it to morning.

SEVEN

Lucas awoke to a hot breath fanning across his face. He blinked open his eyes and found himself nose to nose with Aslan. Daylight peeked around the edges of the curtains, lighting up the small cabin. The dog nudged him and then trotted to the door.

Lucas ran a hand over his face and pushed himself to a seated position, drawing in a deep breath as his muscles and bones protested, giving testament to the uncomfortable night's sleep on the saggy old couch.

Aslan's tail thumped once against the floor as if in admonishment for taking so long to let him out.

Shaking his head, Lucas heaved to his feet. He checked his boots set in front of the now-cold woodstove. Dry enough. He slipped them on, grabbed the leash and attached it to Aslan's collar.

Using caution, Lucas opened the door and they stepped out into the early morning light. He took a moment to assess the area, letting his senses become aware, searching for a threat. The storm had subsided, leaving the world fresh and earthy. He breathed in the crisp air. Patches of blue sky overhead promised better weather. His gaze scanned the clearing rimmed by trees. Yellowed weather-bent grass needed to be mowed. Thankfully, there weren't any signs of Colin. Lucas didn't dare hope The Beast had given up his pursuit. No, more likely the storm and his wounds had forced him to hole up somewhere.

Aslan nudged Lucas again. He quickly unleashed the dog who ran into the woods. He refrained from calling out and telling the dog to not go far. Would Aslan understand him? His mother's dog, a small Pekingese named Ellie, wasn't well-versed in listening to or obeying commands. That dog was a terror. Nothing like this golden retriever.

Lucas moved into the woods to gather some more fire-wood even though they would have to leave soon. But there was no reason for Paige and Kenny to wake up in a cold cabin. Aslan ran ahead as Lucas entered the cabin carrying the wood. Kenny's head appeared over the top of the second-floor landing before he scampered down the ladder.

Kneeling by the woodstove, Lucas set about making a fire.

"Whatcha doing?" Kenny crouched beside Lucas.

Mouth quirking, Lucas replied, "What does it look like I'm doing?"

"Playing with fire."

Kenny's very serious tone had Lucas pausing to look at the kid. "There's a difference between fooling around with a flame and making something useful out it."

Nodding, Kenny rocked back on his socked heels.

"Where is your mom?"

"She's getting pretty." Kenny rose and wandered away.

Clamping his lips together, Lucas refrained from saying aloud that Paige was naturally pretty.

Needing something to do with himself after getting the fire going, Lucas searched the cupboards and found the makings for coffee. He filled a teakettle and set it on the woodstove.

Kenny sat at the table with a stack of blank papers and a couple of pencils next to him.

"What are you doing there?" Lucas took a seat across from him.

"Drawing." Kenny made a face. "I'm not very good."

Lucas took a piece of paper from the stack and picked up one of the pencils. He sketched Kenny hunched over the paper with a pencil in his hand.

"Wow!" Kenny jumped up and came around to look at Lucas's drawing. "You're good."

"Thanks, kid." He slid the paper over. "Yours to keep."

Paige climbed down the ladder. "Good morning. Anyone hungry? I think there might be another can of beans in the cupboard."

"No more beans, Mama. My tummy hurts," Kenny said.

Lucas laughed. "Let's stick with the protein bars for now." He shared a smile with Paige.

"Look what the cowboy drew, Mama," Kenny said holding up the drawing.

Her eyes widened. "That's really…well done." Her gaze, soft and tender, met his. "You're an artist, too?"

His heart did a little skip and he shrugged, uncomfortable with the pleasure her compliment gave him. "I dabble."

Paige's gaze fell to the table and her brow crinkled. "Kenny, where did you find the paper and pens?"

"From your satchel, Mama."

"I'd forgotten," Paige muttered. Her face lost all color, and she gripped the edge of the table.

Lucas stood, concern arcing through him as he reached for her, afraid she was about to faint. "Paige? What's wrong?"

Paige's gaze jerked from the stack of papers and the discarded manila envelope on the floor to meet Lucas's worried eyes. "The night of Donald's—"

She swallowed and glanced at Kenny, unable to bring herself to say the word *assassination*.

"Just before everything happened, Donald had given me a manila envelope to mail. But he'd forgotten to write the name of whom it was to be mailed to. In all the chaos, I just shoved it into my satchel and forgot about it."

Lucas picked up the paper that he'd drawn on and turned it over to stare at what was typed there. His jaw firmed. Anger flashed in his eyes. Paige hurried to his side and gasped as she realized she was looking at part of the missing legal file against the arms dealer, Adam Wayne.

She quickly gathered all the papers and sat down. "I didn't know."

Lucas stood over her, glowering. He couldn't think she had stolen the file, did he?

"Where was this to be sent?" His voice held a hard edge that sent a shiver down her spine.

She bent and scooped up the discarded manila envelope from the floor. She turned it over so he could see the DC address. "I don't recognize it."

"Could that be Eliza Mendez's address?"

Paige set the envelope on the table. "She's a Florida attorney. Doubtful. What do we do with it?"

"We'll deal with this when we are in San Antonio," Lucas said. "Until then, stuff it back in your bag. We need to keep those documents safe."

Lucas crossed the room to the stove and removed the kettle, then headed into the kitchenette.

Her hands shaking, Paige returned the papers to the envelope, noting the drawing of Kenny again. Lucas had captured Kenny's likeness so well.

Before she'd started down the ladder and first seen the two of them, heads bent, pencils moving on the paper, her heart had beat so fast she thought it might come out of her chest. Affection still filled her to the brim. Seeing the two of them together as if they belonged, like a father and son, created a wellspring of both sadness and bittersweetness. Maybe one day she would be able to have someone in her life for Kenny to look up to as a role model.

Lucas couldn't be that man, no matter how attractive she found him or how much she was coming to care for him.

The niggling voice in her head asked, *Why not?*

Because he was too much of a risk-taker. A man who hunted fugitives, protected women from dangerous men and put his life on the line. A man who was willing to die for his job. A man who could break her heart.

Aslan jumped to his feet and let out a high-pitched bark. He raced to the door, his tail up, and growled.

The roar of an engine and tires eating up dirt sent a shudder down Paige's spine. Jolted, she moved protectively to Kenny.

"Take Kenny upstairs," Lucas instructed in a low tone.

Without hesitation, Paige urged Kenny up the ladder. "Go into the bathroom and lock the door."

"Mama? You're coming, too?"

"Go!" She nudged him. He disappeared from sight, and she hurried across the cabin to grab the iron poker leaning against the woodstove.

Lucas grabbed Aslan by the collar. "Paige, upstairs."

"I've got your back," she told him, hefting the poker with both hands.

A strange expression crossed Lucas's face before he dragged Aslan away from the door. "Open the refrigerator door. You two stay behind it."

When she hesitated, he practically growled, "Now."

Lucas moved to the front window and pushed the curtain back enough to peer out.

Deciding it was wisest to do as he instructed, she herded an agitated Aslan to the kitchenette.

Outside a door slammed shut.

Galvanized by the noise, she opened the fridge and hid behind the metal refrigerator door while sending up a fervent plea to God to see them through this ordeal safely.

Adrenaline pumped through Lucas's veins as he pressed his back against the doorjamb. He'd seen a truck and an old man carrying a shotgun head for the cabin. The doorknob wiggled. Then the sound of a key sliding into the lock had tension ratcheting through him.

The door swung open, and Lucas grabbed the edge of it so that it didn't hit him in the face.

"Show yourself!" the man shouted, holding the shotgun with the barrel facing out. "I don't take kindly to squatters on my property."

Lucas quietly stepped from behind the door. After double-checking the man was alone, Lucas placed the barrel of his handgun into the kidney of the big man in front of him. "US marshal. Put down your weapon."

Slowly, the man complied. Lucas kicked the shotgun away. Then he lowered his own weapon. Stepping to the side and keeping his body between the man and the shotgun, Lucas held up his badge. "Deputy US Marshal Lucas Cavendish. And you are?"

"Ted Beale," the man barked. His back was ramrod straight and his chin level. This was a man used to being in charge. His graying hair was shorn tight along the sides. Deep wrinkles bracketed his deep blue eyes. "I own this cabin. Y'all didn't rent it."

Some of the tension left Lucas's body. "No, Ted, we didn't. We stumbled upon this place in the storm last night. We are mighty obliged for the hospitality."

"Are you now?" Ted narrowed his gaze. "What's a deputy US marshal doing here in the middle of the Alabama countryside?"

Fair question. "I'm securing a witness. Paige."

Paige popped up from behind the open refrigerator door. Aslan's head peeked around the side. He let out a bark.

"Well, now," Ted said. "Hello to you, too."

Paige and Aslan came out from behind the refrigerator. "We are sorry for breaking into your cabin," Paige said. "We'll pay the nightly rent."

Ted's gaze bounced between Paige and Lucas. Then back to Paige. "Don't worry about the money." To Lucas, he said, "I take it there are bad people after y'all? How can I help?"

Surprised but grateful for the offer, Lucas said, "There are bad people hunting us. Could you give us a lift into town?"

"Of course. We must stop by and let the Mrs. know that everything's okay. She might have already called the police by now."

Lucas hesitated. He was convinced there was a mole somewhere along the way who had given Colin Richter their whereabouts. "I'd be much obliged if we could stop your wife from calling law enforcement at this juncture. We're trying to stay under the radar."

"Alrighty, then," Ted said. "Let's get y'all into my truck."

"I just need to get my son." Paige scrambled up the ladder to the loft area.

"Son?" Ted's eyes grew round. "You've got a child in tow, too?"

Lucas nodded. "That we do."

A few moments later, Paige and Kenny came down the ladder carrying what meager belongings they'd brought from the car. Both had changed into their clothes from yesterday.

"Mr. Beale, I really hope it's okay that we borrowed some dry clothes for the night. We'll pay you extra for their cleaning."

Ted waved away her offer. "Never you mind that now. Let's get y'all home before Missy can make that phone call."

Lucas bent and picked up the shotgun. His gut told him he could trust this man. He thrust the shotgun back into Ted's hands. "I hope you know how to handle this."

"Yes, Deputy, I do. I've been shooting both as sport and profession since I was a kid." He dipped his chin. "US Army."

Ah, that explained the man's bearings. "Marine gunnery sergeant before Marshals Service."

"Well, isn't that a fine how do you do," Ted said happily. He lifted the shotgun barrel up over his shoulder. "Come along now. Time's a waste'n."

Ted walked out of the cabin, leaving Paige, Kenny and Lucas staring after him.

Lucas chuckled. The man was a character. "You heard the man, let's get a move on."

"Wait," Paige said. "Let me clean up a bit. We don't want to leave him a mess."

"I'm sure he'll understand," Lucas said. "We need to go."

He hustled the trio outside and pulled the door shut behind him.

The sun peeked out behind the gray clouds and cold morning air seeped beneath the collar of Lucas's jacket.

Aslan tugged the leash from Paige's grasp, causing her satchel to slip off her shoulder. She fumbled to catch it, bending down just as the wood of the cabin wall behind her exploded.

"Shooter!" Terror ricocheted through Lucas. He tackled Paige, throwing her to the ground and shielding her with his body. Lucas gestured to Kenny. "Get down."

Ted started up the truck, put it in Reverse, and backed up, turning the wheel so that the truck now provided cover for Kenny, Aslan, Paige and Lucas.

"Hurry, get in." Ted jumped out of the driver's seat and grabbed Kenny. He tucked him into the back of the crew cab. Aslan jumped in without hesitation.

"Lucas?"

Paige's shaking voice registered. Lucas eased off her but kept her shielded with his body. "On three we move. Stay low." Lucas scooted so that he was in front of Paige. "Stay behind me."

Her blue eyes were wide and frightened. She nodded and took a sharp inhale.

"One, two, three," Lucas counted, then as a unit they got to their feet and ran down the porch stairs. More bullets pinged off the truck and embedded themselves in the side of the cabin. Lucas boosted Paige into the back cab. "Stay down!"

Paige clutched her satchel to her and grabbed her child with her other arm. They crouched low on the floorboards behind the front seats.

Ted had his shotgun out and used the front end of the truck for cover. He aimed at the woods. "Where?"

Drawing his own weapon, Lucas took cover behind the bed of the truck and searched the tree line. Sunlight flashed on the scope. "There!" He pointed to the right.

Ted fired off several rounds. Lucas did the same.

"Get us out of here," Lucas shouted.

Ted jumped back into the driver's seat while Lucas jumped over the wheel well into the back bed of the truck. Ted threw the truck in gear, and they took off at a fast clip down the dirt road. The thump and vibration of a flat tire echoed through Lucas. He sent up praises to God that the truck was a dually and had four back tires and could still run even with one flat. More rounds riddled the back of the truck. Lucas chanced a peak over the tailgate to see Colin running after them, firing with his sniper rifle.

The road was bumpy, and Lucas's aim was thrown off as he shot back. Then they were out of range. Colin lifted the rifle to his shoulder, and he stared after them.

Anger burned through Lucas.

Ten minutes later, they pulled into a gated piece of property and stopped in front of a beautiful home with a wraparound porch. A stout gray-haired woman rushed out the front door and met them at the truck.

Great. Now Lucas had four civilians he had to protect. No doubt this was Ted's wife.

"I heard gunfire," the woman said. "I called Aaron. He and his deputies are on their way."

Lucas groaned at the announcement as he climbed out of the back of the truck.

Paige scrambled from the back door of the crew cab. "Are you hurt?"

"Just my ego," he said.

"How did Colin find us?"

"He's a predator tracking his prey." Lucas didn't like being anyone's prey.

"Which means he could track us here?" Paige's voice rose at least two octaves.

"He could." Turning to their host, Lucas said, "Ted, we need wheels. I don't want to put you and your wife in any more danger."

"Missy, this here's Deputy US Marshal Cavendish. Paige, and her son, Kenny. And their dog."

Missy nodded. "We need to get you inside. My nephew Aaron is the county sheriff. He's on his way. You can trust him."

The sound of sirens wailing grew closer.

"Let's get out of the open." Lucas tucked one arm around Paige and the other around Kenny, who had taken hold of Aslan's leash, and hustled them inside behind Missy and Ted.

Glancing over his shoulder, Lucas prayed the sheriff arrived before Colin.

EIGHT

Lucas paced between the living room and kitchen, upset and angry with himself for placing these people in danger. Colin had tracked them through the storm. His injuries hadn't slowed him down enough. Lucas could only thank God the assassin hadn't attacked in the middle of the night. Maybe he hadn't found them until the morning. But he was definitely on their trail now.

Lucas needed backup. The local sheriff and his deputies could only do so much. And Lucas needed to get Paige and Kenny to San Antonio. He needed to call his boss. "Do you have a phone I can use?"

"Use my office. Down the hall first door on your right," Ted told him. He had the shotgun still in his hands. Lucas couldn't blame the man for keeping the weapon close.

The sound of cars coming down the drive had Lucas and Ted hurrying to the windows. Three Baldwin County Sheriff's Broncos arrived in a spray of gravel.

Calling his boss would have to wait. Lucas led the way out the door and flashed his badge at the tall imposing sheriff coming up the porch stairs. The man had broad shoulders and a big brown mustache. He eyed Lucas's badge.

"Uncle Ted, Aunt Missy called saying there was gunfire," Sheriff Aaron Paulson said. "Who shot up your truck?"

"A professional assassin is after my witness," Lucas told him. "We need an escort to San Antonio, Texas."

Concern darkened the sheriff's expression. "I can certainly take you to the county line."

"The quicker we get out of here, the quicker Ted and Missy will be out of danger," Lucas said.

"Maybe," Ted said. "I did see that fellow. He was unforgettable."

Anxiety twisted in Lucas's gut. "You might want to take a vacation. Go away for a while."

"Missy's been wanting to visit her sister in Montana," Ted said. Aaron looked past Lucas toward the open front door. "Where's your witness?"

Missy, Paige, Kenny and Aslan funneled out the door. The dog sniffed the sheriff and then moved to sit beside Kenny, who clung to his mother.

"We're here," Paige said. "Thank you, Sheriff, for coming."

"Aaron, honey, make sure these nice folks get safely to where they're going," Missy said.

"Yes, Aunt Missy," Aaron said. To Lucas, he said, "I'll give Sheriff Swenson in the next county over a heads-up."

"I would suggest you leave your deputies here with your aunt and uncle as a safeguard until they can leave," Lucas told him.

Aaron gave a thoughtful nod. "I'll do that."

A high-pitched whistle rent the air a split second before one of the county Sheriff's Broncos exploded with enough fiery force to rock Lucas back on his heels.

Instinctively, he turned away from the blast, wrapping Paige and Kenny in his arms as a wave of heat buffeted his back. Aslan barked frantically next to them.

The sheriff hit the deck and his two deputies took cover behind Ted's truck, while Ted tugged Missy back into the house.

"Sheriff, we need to get out of here," Lucas shouted. "Or they'll blow the house next, with your aunt and uncle in it."

"Get in my vehicle," the sheriff said and pointed to the nearest vehicle. "That one." He rose and ran for his Bronco.

The two deputies ran to the porch stairs and provided a shield for Lucas as he ushered Paige, Kenny and Aslan to the farthest vehicle.

"My deputies will protect my aunt and uncle," Aaron told them as he jumped into the driver's seat. He only needed a gesture to convey his orders to his men, then grabbed his radio. "We need backup at the Beale place."

"On the floorboards now," Lucas said to Paige and Kenny. Aslan squeezed in next to them. Lucas shut the Bronco's back door on them, his gaze searching for Colin, but the smoke from the destroyed vehicle was too thick. He climbed into the front passenger seat.

The sheriff started the engine and threw the Bronco into gear. He made a quick U-turn and headed back down the drive with the gas pedal to the floor.

Leaning forward in his seat, Lucas kept an eye out for any sign of where Colin was launching his attack. Something bright streaked through the air from the tree line. Jolted by the sight, Lucas shouted, "Incoming. Jog right."

The sheriff twisted the steering wheel, sending the small SUV off the road just as an RPG exploded in the middle of the driveway where they'd been seconds before, sending rocks and debris to pelt the Bronco.

"Who is this guy?" Aaron asked.

"Works for an arms dealer." Lucas wasn't surprised Colin had access to rocket-propelled grenades. He must've called in reinforcements of his own because there was no way he could track them through the woods carrying a grenade launcher. If he'd had it earlier, back at the cabin... Lucas shuddered to think of how close they'd come to dying today.

Were Adam Wayne and Eliza Mendez behind this? Were they supplying Colin with weaponry? Were they nearby?

Even as the thoughts formed, a man Lucas had never seen before stepped out of the tree line ahead of them and began to raise a sniper rifle to his shoulder.

Lucas quickly lowered his window and leaned out to repeatedly shoot at the man, sending him back into the trees as they passed by and sped away from the area.

Lucas sent up a prayer that Colin and his men would, at best, retreat or at least follow the sheriff's Bronco, leaving Ted and Missy alone.

"You'll be safe in here," Sheriff Paulson told Paige as he ushered them into his office in the Baldwin County Sheriff's Department building.

Safe? Would Paige ever feel safe again? During the harrowing ride from the Beales' place to the county seat of Baldwin, she'd held her breath, sure any moment they would be blown to bits.

Quelling her own anxiety, she steered a shaking Kenny to a chair against the interior wall of a well-organized office. A desk faced the door with a bin for inbound correspondence and a bin for outgoing correspondence. A laptop lay closed on the surface with a coaster holding a mug sporting the words *Best Boss Ever* in bold black letters.

With an empathy that came from something other than just training, Aslan pressed himself close to her child. Love for the dog filled her to brimming. She was so thankful to have such a good therapy companion for Kenny.

Lucas squatted down in front of Kenny and reached past the dog to place his hands on her son's knees.

"Deep breaths," Lucas said. "You're doing great." He took off his cowboy hat and placed it on Kenny's head. "Can you take care of this for me while I go talk to the sheriff?"

Kenny sat up straighter, touching the hat with one hand as awe spread over his face. "Yes, sir."

Paige marveled at how good Lucas was with her son. Were all marshals trained to soothe witnesses in the same way? Or was he just remarkable?

Since she had no one to compare him to, she decided to take a metaphorical step back. Her senses were heightened, and her emotions were running rampant with anger because the assassin had found them. Not to mention her fear that he would kill them. Each time a bullet whizzed close, or something went kaboom, her heart stuttered in her chest, and she prayed that God would spare them. They'd made it safely to the sheriff's department. And she was grateful. But she was still very scared.

Lucas rose and turned to her. "I'll be back in a moment. I need to call for reinforcements."

She gripped his sleeve. "Please check on Ted and Missy. If anything happened to them—"

"I will." Lucas covered her hand with his, threading his fingers through hers.

Warmth seeped into her cold skin and spread up her arm and through her chest. He was a tether she needed to cling to in the chaos of this overwhelming storm. What would she do without him?

The question was enough to force her to relinquish her hold on him and extract her hand. She needed to let him do his job. She needed to remember she couldn't rely on anyone else, not fully. He was here for a reason and a specific amount of time that had an expiration date. She was attaching too much to his presence and doing so would only hurt in the end.

"Shouldn't you bring in the FBI? Maybe even the National Guard, to help find Colin and his minions?"

Her gaze rested on her son. For his sake, she needed

Lucas to track down the fugitives and put them behind bars. That was the only way she and her son would ever be able to live a normal life. "They have to be stopped," she said emphatically.

Lucas reached out to tuck a lock of her hair behind her ear, his fingers grazing across her skin. A heightened mix of delight and searing pain cascaded through her. It had been too long since anyone, especially a man, had offered a kind touch. She'd convinced herself she didn't need anyone other than Kenny. But as she looked deep into Lucas's brown eyes, she could feel herself falling. And wanting. And yearning.

Alarm bells went off in her head. She couldn't fall for this man. She couldn't want him. And she absolutely couldn't yearn for him.

If only her heart and her head could agree.

"I'm going to do everything in my power to keep you and Kenny safe."

The words *trust me* hung in the air between them even though he hadn't uttered them.

She did trust this man. Trusted in his promise to keep them safe. Trusted him to make her and Kenny a priority.

Trusted him with her heart.

And that scared her almost as much as the assassin chasing them.

Time to retreat.

It took all of Lucas's willpower not to pull Paige into his arms and soothe away the frightened, cornered look in her eyes. He could only imagine the toll the horrors of the past few days were taking on her and yet, she was holding it together. Her quiet strength and resilience were both admirable and alluring. What would life be like if they'd met under different circumstances? Would he have asked her out? Would she have accepted? Would the glow of attraction have burned as bright?

But the questions were moot.

He stepped back and gave a nod. "I'll be right back."

Closing the door behind him, he breathed through the constriction in his chest. *Get a grip!*

Paige was off-limits for so many reasons. His assignment was to protect her and her son and deliver them safely to San Antonio. Then the two would disappear into the WITSEC program and he'd return his focus to bringing Colin Richter, Adam Wayne and Eliza Mendez to justice.

Lucas found the sheriff and several of his deputies coordinating with the local police. As he stepped into the conference-style room, all eyes turned to stare at him. The saying "a fish out of water" came to mind. He was the anomaly here. The outsider. It would take more than his badge for these men and women to trust him. And vice versa.

He met the sheriff's gaze and said, "I need to make a private call."

Aaron nodded and turned to his men. "Get out there. Search every inch of those woods from here to the Beale place. Find those men and their weapons."

To Lucas, Aaron gestured with his head. "Follow me."

Lucas followed the sheriff down the hallway to a dark office. Aaron entered and turned on the light. The stark glow of a single bulb showed an empty desk with empty bookshelves behind it.

"No one will bother you in here," the sheriff said. "You can use the landline. But you should have a cell signal now."

"Perfect. Any news on how Ted and Missy are?"

"Safe, unharmed. Those jokers after you didn't bother them once we left. Aunt Missy and Uncle Ted are already on their way to Montana," Aaron told him. "But the bad guys haven't resurfaced."

Hence, why the sheriff was having the show of force beat the bushes in the woods. Lucas itched to join in the search, but his priority had to be Paige and Kenny.

The sheriff left the office, closing the door behind him.

Lucas sat at the desk and called the San Antonio US Marshals' office on the burner phone he'd bought. He asked to speak to Gavin.

"Marshal Armstrong," his boss answered.

"It's Cavendish," Lucas said. "We had some trouble." He explained, working to keep the trauma from his voice. His boss didn't need to know the upsetting situation was taking a toll on him. "I need those reinforcements. We're at the Baldwin County Sheriff's Department. We're safe here. But I don't know for how long. I need to get Paige and her son out of here. Colin is hot on our trail with military-grade help. The sheriff can get us to the state line."

"Understood. I'll send Brian and Sera to meet you," Gavin said. "Just so you know, I've received abundant calls from Homeland Security and the FBI. Special Agent McIntosh and his boss are all over us, wanting to know what's happening. Especially in light of Adam Wayne's release. The man has dropped out of sight." The news hit Lucas like a punch to the gut. He was glad he was sitting. A deep burning anger sluiced through him. It wasn't right or fair that the task force's hard work had been undone so brutally and that Adam had gone to the ground, like the weasel he was. No doubt hiding in some basement bunker where he thought he'd be safe. But Lucas and Paige had the ammunition to put Adam Wayne back behind bars. "Sir, I have—"

"We'll talk when you get here," Gavin cut him off. "I'll speak to the FBI but I'll leave Barlow to you." Gavin hung up.

Lucas blew out an aggravated breath. He really wanted to share the news that they'd found the case file with Gavin. All in good time. Heeding his boss's directive, Lucas dialed James's private number.

"Speak," James barked.

"Sir, it's Cavendish," Lucas said. "I have news that will make your day."

"Really? Spill," James said, impatience threading his voice.

"I have a hard copy of Donald Lessing's case file against Adam Wayne." Lucas waited, expecting some sort of jubilation from James.

After a tense pause, James said, "Come again?"

"I can hardly believe it myself," Lucas told him about finding the file in Paige's satchel and how she came to be in possession of it.

"Have you read it?"

"Not yet, sir." Lucas remembered the DC address on the manila envelope. "Lessing intended this copy to go to someone in DC."

"Give me the information. I'll run the address. You've enough on your plate with the witness," James said.

Surprised by the courtesy, Lucas relayed the address he'd memorized.

"Got it," James said, his voice taking on an intense note. "You can't let the file out of your possession. And don't show it to anyone."

"Sir?" Lucas didn't feel right keeping the information from Gavin.

"I'm afraid we have a leak somewhere and I need to plug it before we go public with the fact we can proceed with the case against Wayne," James said. "Do you understand?"

"Okay." Unease skated across Lucas's neck. "I'll make sure to keep it safe with the witness."

"Excellent," James said. "Keep them together. If anything else comes up, contact me pronto."

"Will do." Lucas hung up. He didn't like the idea of a mole in their midst. Who? Someone from the task force? Another agency?

He didn't want the incriminating file to fall into the wrong hands. He would keep the documents close until he could hand them over to James. Right now, Colin was after them because Paige could identify him as the killer of her boss. But if Colin or Adam Wayne realized the depth of the threat Paige presented to them, unquestionably Colin would double his efforts to eliminate her.

Leaving the sheriff's station in a convoy of SUVs, Lucas's nerves stretched taut with each mile as they made their way to the rendezvous point where his fellow US marshals would meet them.

The transfer from the sheriff's vehicle to the black SUV driven by Deputy US Marshal Brian Forrester went smoothly.

Keeping a close vigil on their surroundings, Lucas breathed a sigh of relief as he finally settled in the back of the SUV with Paige and Kenny. Aslan was in the back compartment, sitting up where he watched out the rear window. Deputy US Marshal Sera Morales-O'Brien rode in the front passenger seat.

The armor-plated vehicle ate up the road as they motored through Louisiana and into Texas.

Somewhere along the way, Kenny had settled his head against Lucas's chest, creating a warm spot near his heart. Paige had rolled up some clothing to use as a pillow and was getting some rest. Lucas knew he should do the same, but his senses were still on high alert.

Careful not to wake Kenny, Lucas shifted and set the boy

so that he leaned against his mother. Paige briefly opened her eyes to wrap her arms around her son and give Lucas a sleepy smile. His heart pumped. What was he going to do when he had to release these two forever?

That was something he couldn't think about. Shouldn't think about. There was no future where they were in his life. He was a loner, not willing to form a lifelong commitment he might not be able to fulfill. So why was he even having these thoughts?

He sat forward to quietly address his fellow marshals. "When we reach town, you can drop me off at my apartment and take Paige and Kenny to Armstrong's." He needed a change of clothes, a shower and a shave. He trusted his friends more than anyone with the assignment.

Sera twisted in her seat to stare at him. "We'll *all* go to your apartment. Then we'll *all* go to the Armstrong ranch. Richter's after you just as much as he is after Paige and Kenny."

Lucas's gut clenched at the truth in the words. But he could protect himself. In fact, he relished Colin coming after him. Just him. It was past time for them to settle their score. One way or another. Preferably, Colin ended up in handcuffs. Or in the ground.

"I concur," Paige's sleepy voice wrapped around Lucas. "Where you go, we go. We're safer together."

"Yeah, what the lady said," Brian said, his voice low and firm.

Lucas sat back, marveling at the odd twist his life had taken. He didn't do emotional attachments.

But somehow, he'd found himself attached to this group of people and he couldn't deny he was grateful.

He prayed nothing would befall his friends or this woman and child he was coming to care for.

NINE

Paige hugged Kenny close as the marshals ushered them through the entrance of an apartment complex on a tree-lined street in San Antonio. She would've liked to have had time to stretch her legs a little but understood the need to get out of the open.

The deputy marshal named Brian took Aslan for a walk. *To secure the perimeter.*

A measure that sent a sliver of fear into Paige. She wanted to ask if it was safe for him to take Aslan but then decided the dog would make a ruckus if there were trouble. She prayed there'd be no trouble.

Lucas led the way past a bank of mailboxes recessed into a wall and up two flights of stairs to his apartment. Nervous flutters raced through Paige with each step. There was no reason for her to be anxious. But for some reason, anticipating this glimpse into the life of the man guarding her was both exciting and filled her with trepidation. Would they be walking into a messy bachelor pad? Or was Lucas a clean and tidy person, having the type of home where she and Kenny would have to be careful not to touch anything?

Lucas unlocked the door, his hand on his weapon, and put his finger to his lips.

Sera Morales-O'Brien, the other deputy US marshal, tugged Paige and Kenny away from the door and sandwiched them against the wall with her in front of them like a shield. Her hand was also on her sidearm.

Nerves firing like Fourth of July sparklers, Paige held her breath and tucked Kenny behind her.

Did Lucas believe the assassin had anticipated their return to San Antonio and was waiting inside the apartment? Was that even possible?

Lucas entered the dark apartment and Paige sent up a silent prayer for protection.

A moment later, lights glowed from the interior of the apartment and Lucas called out, "Clear."

Sera let out a breath and visibly relaxed her stance. "We can go in." She gestured. "After you."

Paige and Kenny entered the apartment and several things hit Paige at once. The apartment was neat and orderly, everything in its place, with a surprisingly light and airy feel to the living room, kitchen and dining space. It wasn't stark but rather had a lived-in vibe. A comfortable-looking futon sat beneath a large painting that took up most of the soft colored living room wall. The seascape watercolor drew her forward.

"Southern Italy," Lucas said. "Puglia."

She glanced at him, liking his strong profile. "Have you been?"

A smile curved his lips. "I have."

"It's lovely." She tore her gaze away from his mouth and back to the framed art on the wall. "I wish we were there right now. Then maybe this nightmare wouldn't be happening."

Lucas squeezed her shoulder. "You'll have time to see the world. I'll make sure of it." His gaze captured and held hers for a moment, then he dropped his hand from her shoulder and stepped away. "I'm going to go freshen up."

Paige watched him stride away until he disappeared into what she assumed was a master bedroom.

In the kitchen, Sera and Kenny were raiding the refrigerator. From the looks of it, they were making sandwiches. The smell of tuna made Paige's stomach grumble with hunger. It had been at least six hours since their last meal. And even then, she'd barely eaten a quarter of her hamburger from the fast-food joint they had buzzed through on the way to San Antonio.

Paige stepped into the kitchen. "What can I do to help?"

Kenny stood on a dining room chair at the counter. Sera had given him the task of spreading mayonnaise on slices of bread.

"See if there's any pickles, capers or something to dress up this tuna salad," Sera said with a smile.

Glad to have something to occupy her hands and her mind, Paige rummaged through the refrigerator and the cupboards until she found a jar of dill pickles. She found a cutting board and a knife perfect for chopping up the pickles. "How long have you known Lucas?"

The question popped out before she considered how the query might appear to the other woman. Was she fishing for information on her handsome protector? Yes. Yes, she was. Only because it seemed right to understand him. To bolster her trust in him. Certainly not because she was attracted.

And maybe pigs would one day sprout wings and fly.

Paige suppressed a laugh at her own absurdity.

"We've worked together for a little over a year now," Sera replied. "He's been a good addition to our team."

So not long. She remembered Lucas saying he'd been a bronc rider and then a marine before joining the Marshal service. "How long have you been a deputy marshal?"

"Six years." Sera reached for the diced pickles and put

them into the bowl with the tuna. "I went through the police academy with my boss's son, Jace, and Brian."

Noting the rose gold band circling Sera's ring finger, Paige asked, "You're married?"

A smile spread across Sera's face, lighting up her whole expression. She pushed back stray strands of dark hair that had escaped from her braid. "I am. He's with the DEA— Drug Enforcement Administration. We worked on a task force together and well, fell in love."

"The same task force Lucas was on?"

"No. A different one. Though if another task force is formed to take down Adam Wayne, my husband and I are both itching to get on it."

Paige couldn't fathom the drive toward danger these people possessed.

"Is it hard doing your job and being married?"

Sera slanted Paige a glance that sent a rush of heat to settle in Paige's cheeks. The speculation in Sera's eyes was undeniable.

"No more so than any other career, I would suppose," Sera said. "Yes, we both have dangerous jobs. Life is dangerous. But we also trust each other and know that we are surrounded by a good team. We have faith and that makes all the difference."

"Faith does make a difference," Paige agreed. "But it doesn't make it hurt any less when tragedy happens."

Sera paused and turned to fully face Paige. "God never promised us a pain-free life. In fact, the opposite. The Bible says there will be trials of many kinds. But clinging to your faith despite the circumstances, or because of the circumstances, is how my husband and I choose to live."

Paige liked that philosophy but deep inside she acknowledged how hard it was to cling to faith in times of crisis.

But she supposed the acknowledgment said more about her than it did about faith.

"Trouble comes and trouble goes," Sera said. "But love remains and is worth the risk."

Paige liked this woman. She wished there would be time for them to become deeper friends. An impossible wish.

Still, the yearning to have had someone like Sera in her life when she'd been dealing with her husband's death ached within Paige. Someone who wouldn't sugarcoat the truth. Oh, sure, people had been sympathetic and empathized with her, but she could see their pity and had felt the shame. Her husband's recklessness had been well-known in their circle of friends. Paige had a feeling Sera wouldn't have made excuses for his actions. Something Paige had done in the beginning until the denial and anger gave way to acceptance.

Kenny tugged at Paige's sleeve, drawing her attention. "Can I have one of those?" He pointed to a basket on the shelf that would normally have held fruit but instead held small bags of corn chips.

"I'm sure Lucas wouldn't mind," Paige said.

Kenny snagged one of the bags and hopped off the chair. Paige smiled as she watched Kenny head to the dining room table where he spread a napkin and sprinkled the chips out.

There was a soft knock at the front door.

Paige stiffened, her gaze seeking Sera's.

"Brian," Sera said as she wiped her hands on a towel and then headed to the door with her hand on her holstered weapon.

So not as confident in her statement as she wanted Paige to believe.

Paige moved to where Kenny sat and stood in front of him. She wasn't going to take chances with her son.

Sera opened the door to reveal Brian with Aslan sitting

next to him. Brian reached down and unleashed the dog, giving him a good pat on the head before saying, "Release."

Aslan bound into the room, straight to her. He nudged her with his nose, then circled around her to put his head on Kenny's lap. Kenny scratched him behind the ears.

"Kenny, before you touch your corn chips again you need to wash your hands," Paige said.

"Oh, Mom," Kenny whined. "Aslan's not dirty."

Paige raised an eyebrow and Kenny sighed heavily. He slipped off the chair and hurried back to the kitchen sink where Brian was in the process of washing his hands. Brian lifted Kenny and held him so he could wash his hands. Gratitude for the kind gesture filled Paige. These were good people.

Sera placed a plate of tuna salad sandwiches on the table. Then she looked at Paige, and said, "Would you knock on Lucas's door and let him know we have food ready?"

Paige's heart jumped in her throat. The two marshals sat down at the table. Each had moved their chair so that they flanked Kenny, leaving the other two chairs open across from them. The marshals couldn't be matchmaking, could they?

No, they were just being cautious in protecting her son. And that's what she wanted. She hustled down the hall to the closed door and knocked. From within, she heard Lucas say, "Come in."

She hesitated, her hand on the doorknob. She released the knob and tucked her hands behind her back. "Food is ready."

Before she could turn away, Lucas opened the door. He stood there in a fresh shirt and dark denim jeans. He held a pair of socks in his hand. His dark hair was damp and curled at the edges. He'd shaven and his brown eyes were warm. Her heart pumped. Attraction zinged through her.

"Almost ready," Lucas said as he headed back to the bed, sat on the edge and pulled on a sock.

Unsure what she should do, Paige lingered in the doorway, taking in the room. Lucas's inner sanctuary was not as light and airy as the rest of his apartment. Deep blues and slashes of purple against mahogany furniture gave the room a regal and masculine look.

A collection of framed photos on the wall next to a window drew her gaze. Almost as if drawn by an invisible tether, she moved forward to look at the images.

"My family," Lucas said.

She studied the photos of Lucas's family and the progression of his parents' wedding photos to pictures through the years, showing their children, including Lucas, a dark-haired imp with a great smile. He reminded her of the way Kenny was when he was happy. There were wedding photos of his siblings and then pictures of children that resembled Lucas and his siblings. She lingered on the images of Lucas graduating high school and in his marine uniform. So handsome. In the photo of him receiving his gold marshal's badge, pride shone brightly in his eyes and in the expression of the gray-haired man standing next to him. There was a picture of Lucas with Sera, Brian and another man. They were mugging for the camera in a way people who knew each other well did.

An inexplicable sadness enveloped Paige. She and Kenny would never be a part of this man's life. Would never meet this family that clearly adored each other. Be friends with his friends.

The future in WITSEC was unknown and uncertain for her and Kenny. Where would they end up? Would she ever be comfortable letting anyone into their life?

Why couldn't they just stay here, cocooned in safety with Lucas?

Because reality wouldn't be denied. An assassin was

after them. And disappearing was the only way to ensure she and her son survived.

Abruptly, she headed for the door. "We better hurry if we're going to get our share."

Lucas stared after Paige, wondering what she thought of his family and of the inner sanctuary of his home. Having her here felt foreign and yet, right. He liked having Paige and Kenny in his life, but he would do well to remember they were only temporary inhabitants. Becoming attached and forming bonds with the lovely widow and her son would only prove hurtful for them all.

The quicker he got them to the Armstrong ranch the better.

He grabbed a fresh set of boots and cowboy hat off the peg on the wall. He hooked his badge to his belt loop and his holster to his hip. He grabbed a flak vest and a US marshal jacket out of the closet. He needed to put on his armor, both figuratively and literally.

By the time Lucas entered the dining room, there were two sandwiches left on a plate.

"We saved those for you." Paige met his gaze. The wistfulness in her eyes stole his breath. "Do you mind if I give Kenny a quick shower?"

"Of course, please," Lucas told her, glad his voice worked past the lump in his throat. "There are fresh linens in the hall closet."

He watched Paige usher Kenny into the guest bathroom. Aslan lay down in front of the closed bathroom door.

"I like that lady," Brian said. "She's smart and has a good sense of humor."

"It's too bad her life's been blown up the way it has," Sera said.

Lucas focused on his friends and resisted squirming under

their speculative gazes. "We have to get the pair into WIT-SEC ASAP. The sooner they are relocated under new identities, the faster we can focus our energies on hunting down Colin Richter and putting Adam Wayne behind bars."

"Are you sure WITSEC is the right move here?" Sera tilted her head. "We are taking them to the Armstrong ranch. They'll be safe there. Once we bring Colin to justice and he's put behind bars, he won't be able to do anything to harm her or her son."

"We can't take that chance with their lives," Lucas said. He didn't relish sending them away to never be able to contact them again. He would not be their handler. It had to be someone who wasn't emotionally involved. Because he was struggling to stay detached.

After cleaning up what little mess there was from the meal, Lucas checked in with their boss.

"Everything is ready at the ranch," Gavin said. "Victoria is expecting all of you. We don't have any Camp Strong guests right now."

The Armstrong ranch was named Camp Strong because Victoria Armstrong periodically ran a camp for at-risk youths. There were several tiny cabins on the property for the campers. Gavin Armstrong had taken every precaution he could to ensure his wife and those on the ranch stayed safe. There were very few people who even knew Camp Strong was attached to Marshal Gavin Armstrong. The ranch was under his wife's maiden name. It had belonged to her family long before she met Gavin. Their son, Jace, also a deputy US marshal, worked out of the Portland, Oregon, office where his wife, Abby, was a bank manager. Victoria and Gavin had taken all of the deputies under their wing and Lucas was grateful for their care.

Paige and Kenny came out of the bathroom. Aslan trotted into the living room behind Kenny, who looked freshly scrubbed and his hair damp. The child climbed up onto the futon and snuggled with Aslan.

Paige joined the others in the kitchen. "What's the plan?"

"We're all done here," Lucas said. "We'll load into the SUV and head out to the ranch. It's about an hour's drive outside of the city."

A dubious expression crossed Paige's face and she glanced toward where Kenny had fallen asleep on the futon.

"I don't think any of us are up for another hour in the car," Paige said. "We're safe here, right?"

"For the time being," Lucas said. "But the plan has always been to go straight to the Armstrong ranch. You should already be there by now."

"But we're here," Paige said. "Kenny needs to sleep. He and I can share the futon. It pulls out, right?"

"It does, but—"

Brian put a hand on Lucas's shoulder, cutting him off.

"Let the child and his mother sleep," Brian said. "We can come back in the morning and take you out to the ranch. I'll square it away with the boss. And I already secured SAPD patrol. There's an officer standing guard in front and one in back."

Lucas was grateful for his friend's consideration and strategic planning. He considered Paige, noting the dark circles under her eyes and the weariness in her posture. He wouldn't ask more of her tonight. And he wasn't about to let Paige and Kenny sleep on the futon. To Brian, he said, "Be back in the morning, eight a.m."

Sera and Brian exchanged satisfied nods.

"Duncan will thank you," Sera said, referring to her husband, DEA agent Duncan O'Brien.

"Adele as well," Brian said, referring to his wife, a federal court district judge whom he'd met when protecting her last year after a deranged bomber blew up the courthouse.

"Yeah, yeah," Lucas waved off their comments. "Tell your spouses hello and thank you. We'll see you in the morning."

After Brian and Sera left, Lucas locked the door and checked all the windows to make sure they were secure before he moved back into the living room.

"You're not sleeping on the futon," Lucas told her. "I'll sleep out here. You two will take my bed."

Paige smiled at him gratefully. "If you're sure—"

Lucas chuckled softly at her attempt to be polite when he could tell sleeping on the futon was not appealing.

"I insist. I'll carry him into the room," he told her.

Paige nodded and hurried ahead of him into his bedroom. Aslan watched as Lucas tucked his arm under Kenny's knees and one around his shoulders while protecting his neck. He lifted him to his chest. The dog stayed at their side as Lucas carried Kenny into the bedroom. Paige had turned down the bed and the only light illuminating the room came from the master bath. Lucas laid Kenny onto the mattress and tucked the covers up around him.

Paige walked to the bedroom door. Lucas followed her. He'd sleep in his clothes. He needed to be ready for anything.

"You have an extra blanket and pillow for yourself?" she asked, voice soft.

Her thoughtful question wrapped around his heart. "I do. In the hall closet."

She placed a hand on his chest, her palm burning through the fabric of his shirt and into his skin. "You're a good man, Lucas. Kenny and I wouldn't have survived this long without you."

He captured her hand and kissed her knuckles. "Glad to be of service," he murmured.

She tilted her head, her eyes assessing in the dim light. "Is that all it is? You being of service?"

His heart thumped against his rib cage. The truth danced on his tongue. But how could he tell her the truth that he was coming to care for her when soon they would be parted for good? It wouldn't be fair to either of them.

"I'm doing my job, Paige," he said decisively.

"And you're doing it well." She moved closer.

He straightened his spine.

She lifted on tiptoe, her intent clear.

His mind said to step back, but his heart said to take her in his arms.

The decision was taken from him when she caressed his cheek and pulled him close. Her soft lips landed on his jaw.

Turning and capturing her lips with his own would be the most natural thing in the world.

Not fair. The refrain echoed through his brain.

His heart wouldn't allow the kiss to go on unacknowledged.

He lifted his hand and caressed her cheek. He bent forward to kiss her petal soft cheekbone, but she turned her head and captured his lips.

He froze. His mind and his heart detonated like canon fire, but then he gave over to the longing crowding through his lungs. His arms snaked around her, drawing her closer.

She clung to him as they both deepened the kiss.

When they broke apart, he dropped his forehead to hers. "It's not fair," he murmured, giving voice to the refrain still echoing through his brain.

"I've found that life is rarely fair," she murmured. "We better get some sleep."

She stepped back, releasing him and forcing him to release her. He gave a sharp nod, though his boots felt like they were filled with sand as he walked out of the room and she shut the door behind him.

TEN

The low rumble of Aslan's growl disrupted the quiet night and sent an alarm through Lucas. He'd taken the dog out for a quick respite and to check in with the officers watching his apartment building. The hairs at the back of his neck stood on end. His hand went to his weapon as he slowly turned, his gaze scanning the inky night for the threat.

A man emerged from the shadows near the building. The crackle of the radio brought swift relief as the officer stepped into the soft glow of the parking lot light. He held his hands up and then slowly reached for his mike on his shoulder.

"Dispatch, Officer Sloan reporting in," he said. "All quiet." With confident strides, the officer walked forward. "Deputy, what are you doing out here?"

Lucas reined in his exasperation and anger and managed to say in a reasonably calm voice, "What were you doing?"

"Stretching my legs," the officer replied. "And checking to make sure that the doors and windows are secure."

Though Lucas couldn't fault him for the security measures, his heart still beat too rapidly in his throat for comfort. He forced himself to relax his stance.

"The dog and I are heading back in," Lucas said. "Please alert me if there's any trouble."

The officer nodded and then opened the door of his vehicle. "I realize you marshals tend to be lone wolves, but you have to trust that the SAPD is doing their job. No one's getting in that building tonight who doesn't belong."

Lucas nodded his head in acknowledgment and chose not to respond to the crack about being lone wolves. He tended to have that bent but, time and time again, he'd learned the lesson of teamwork. First in the Marines, then on the task force, and now as a marshal. "Good to know. We'll sleep better tonight."

Lucas led Aslan back around to the front of the building and entered. After checking his mailbox, which was empty, he then moved to the shadow of the staircase where he and Aslan stood watch for several long minutes. He could see the SAPD officer at the curb. But the interior of the cruiser was dark as it should be. There was no movement on the street.

Yet, Lucas had an awful feeling deep in the pit of his gut that danger was coming, like a tidal wave, intending to wreak havoc in its wake. He had to make sure Paige and Kenny didn't drown.

He led Aslan upstairs to his apartment and locked the door behind them, putting the chain across the doorjamb. After Aslan drank some water, Lucas put him back into the room where Paige and Kenny slept. Knowing he needed to get some shut-eye or he would be no use to anyone tomorrow, Lucas sat on the futon with his weapon in his lap and the lights out. He closed his eyes and breathed deeply, allowing his body and mind to rest.

Paige awoke to the smell of coffee and bacon. Her stomach grumbled, forcing her out of the warm soft bed. Kenny stirred but didn't awaken. After quickly freshening up, she changed out of the T-shirt she'd worn to bed back into the clothes she'd arrived in. She and Kenny would need to go shopping soon. They both were out of clean clothes. And even those they'd had, when washed, wouldn't last them more than a couple of days.

She ventured into the main part of the apartment in bare feet, following her hunger to the kitchen where Lucas was busy flipping bacon. She pulled up short at the sight of him wearing a black apron over jeans and a button-down shirt with a set of tongs in his hands. He was so handsome and kind and caring. Her heart did a little jig.

"How do you like your eggs?" Lucas asked with a smile, his brown eyes warm and inviting. "You should get Kenny up. As soon we eat, we're heading to headquarters."

Blinking away the attraction zinging through her system, she said, "I thought we were going to the Armstrong ranch?"

"We will. The FBI special agent in charge has arrived at the marshal's office. He wants to talk to you."

Best to get everything over with as soon as possible and disappear. As much as she hated to think of never seeing Lucas again, for her and Kenny's sake, it had to be done.

"Scrambled is fine," she said. "We'll be back in a moment."

She hustled to the bedroom where Kenny and Aslan were both awake. Kenny had unlocked her new phone and was watching a cartoon on YouTube.

"Put that away, sweetie," she said. "Lucas has breakfast ready. We need to eat and then get going. So, hustle getting dressed, and come out to the kitchen."

Kenny closed out the program and tossed the phone to the edge of the bed before he scurried into the bathroom, shutting the door behind him.

Paige was grateful he hadn't had another seizure and prayed that he wouldn't.

She put on her socks and shoes. Then stripped the bed

of the sheets, piling them on the floor to go in the laundry. She'd packed what meager belongings they had by the time Kenny came out of the bathroom, dressed.

They joined Lucas in the dining room where he had set plates and was serving up eggs. A pile of bacon sat on a serving dish in the center of the table. Glasses of orange juice waited.

Paige and Kenny sat at the table. Lucas took off the apron and then also sat down.

"Can I say the blessing?" Kenny asked, holding out his hands to his mother and Lucas.

Paige grasped her son's hand and looked at Lucas. Without hesitation, Lucas folded his big hand around Kenny's. "Please do."

Tender affection filled Paige as she and Lucas shared a smile.

"Dear Lord, please bless this food to our bodies and our bodies to your service, amen," Kenny said.

Paige squeezed her son's hand and then picked up her fork. The eggs were fluffy and delicious. For a long moment, none of them made a noise as they ate. A testament to their hunger.

Sated, Paige said, "When we are in town, Kenny and I need to stop at a store to get some more supplies and clothes."

Lucas wiped his mouth with his napkin and gave a slow nod. "After we turn the file in and you are deposed we'll make the stop. There's a huge multipurpose store on the way out of town."

"Great. Though I'm not sure how I'll pay for what we need." Flutters of anxiety took flight in her stomach. "I probably shouldn't use my credit cards."

"Correct," Lucas confirmed. "I'll take care of it."

"You shouldn't have to spend your money on us," she protested.

"The witness protection program has funds allocated for this very purpose," he replied.

Mollified yet not at all comfortable with what was essentially charity, she sighed. "I don't like this."

He gave her a sympathetic smile. "You'll get through this. I promise."

If only getting through this ordeal didn't entail giving up her identity and relocating to an unknown place where she and Kenny knew no one.

Brian and Sera arrived to take them to the Marshals' headquarters.

After making sure Aslan had a chance to use the lawn, they piled into Sera and Brian's SUV and headed into downtown San Antonio. The building wasn't far from the San Antonio courthouse. They parked in the back, hurried inside and went through the security measures, then were quickly ushered to the offices on the second floor.

A tall handsome silver-haired man met them.

"Mrs. Walsh, I'm Marshal Gavin Armstrong," the man said, holding out his hand.

Paige shook his hand, noting that like Lucas, Marshal Armstrong's hands were rough, giving testament to the hard work these men engaged in. But he also owned a ranch, so of course he would have workingman's hands.

"Thank you, Marshal Armstrong, for everything your deputies have done to keep us safe," Paige said.

"All in a day's work," Gavin replied. "Now, if you will follow me, the FBI wants to formally depose you before we fill out the paperwork for witness protection."

Her heart rate ticked up. She turned to Lucas, and said, "Can you occupy Kenny and Aslan?"

Lucas frowned. "I'd like to be in there with you."

"I'm sure I will be safe with Marshal Armstrong. Kenny trusts you. He needs you."

For a second, panic flashed in Lucas's gaze, then his jaw firmed. He gave a slow nod. "Of course."

Paige shoved her satchel purse at him. "Can you do something with this?"

Understanding that she wanted him to be in charge of the file held within the bag flared in his expression and he nodded. "Yes, I will. Come on, Kenny. Let's go raid the vending machine."

An automatic mom sort of protest rose in Paige's throat, but she swallowed it back. It wouldn't harm the boy to have some snacks. "For the road," she couldn't resist saying.

Lucas and Kenny both paused and looked at each other, then looked back over their shoulders at her. The twin expression of exasperation made her knees weak. How had Kenny and Lucas bonded so thoroughly in such a short time?

The two shrugged and continued on their way.

The low chuckle of the marshal snapped Paige's attention back to the man in charge of this whole operation. She gave him a sheepish grin. "Sorry. Force of habit."

"Oh, I get it. I have a son myself."

"Who is also a deputy, from what I understand," she replied.

"He is that." Gavin's smile was genuine. "I'm very proud of him. He turned out well."

"I'm worried about Kenny," she confessed. "With us going into witness protection, how will I ever allow anyone into our lives again?"

Empathy and sympathy mingled in the marshal's expression. "It's hard, I'm not going to lie to you. But you'll figure it out. There will be teachers and coaches who will be none the wiser of your past. But they will still have a positive influence on your son."

"I pray so," she muttered. "We'll never see any of you again, will we?"

This time the marshal's gaze turned speculative. "No one in this office. You will have a handler out of the office closest to wherever you end up. The contact will be minimal and only if there's a credible threat to you, or Kenny."

"Right." But a question remained. She halted and stared through the glass into a room where Agent McIntosh and another older man waited. They both wore dark suits, red ties and white shirts. If she had seen them in the halls of the justice department, she would've thought they were lawyers.

She put a hand on Marshal Armstrong's arm. "If you bring Colin Richter to justice and put Adam Wayne and his lawyer behind bars," she said softly. "Then would Kenny and I be able to resume our normal lives?"

"Not without risk," he said.

She understood that bad people did bad things from behind bars. "But once they are arrested, tried and put in jail, what good would harming me do?"

Even as she said the words, the thought of revenge as a motivator slammed into her brain. She didn't know if she could live this way. The constant tension and fear.

"Let's take one hurdle at a time," Gavin said gently.

Good advice. And best if she heeded it. With a sigh, she entered the room and the two FBI agents stood.

Lucas ran out of coins and dollar bills for the vending machine, but not before he and Kenny had picked pretty much everything that tasted good and was unhealthy. "We're not going to eat these all at once, right?"

"Right. Mama would not be happy," Kenny agreed, his arms filled with cookies, chips and cupcakes.

Lucas chuckled as he led Kenny to his workspace. He set Paige's satchel down on the desk and dug out the file in the manila envelope from the depths of the bag. To Kenny, he said, "Pick one snack for now."

Kenny laid out the treats across the desk in a very serious manner. "Yes, sir."

For moment, Lucas watched Kenny as he seriously debated which of the treats he wanted first. It was fascinating to watch how the boy's mind worked. He pushed the chips away.

Lucas arched an eyebrow.

Kenny said, "Afternoon snacks."

"Good to know."

While Kenny continued to debate his choices, Lucas picked up the manila envelope. It was time to share it with Gavin despite James's directive not to show the file to anyone. Lucas's loyalty had to be with his current boss. "Kenny, don't move. I'll be right over there." Lucas pointed to Gavin's office.

"Okey dokey," Kenny said without breaking his focus from the snacks.

Taking the file with him, Lucas headed to Gavin's office to show him what they'd found but Gavin was on the phone.

Gavin put his hand over the receiver and said to Lucas, "Give me five."

Lucas nodded his understanding and bit back his impatience as he retreated and pulled up a chair to the other side of his desk where Kenny ate a cupcake.

"Would you like some?" Kenny held up the chocolate and white icing confection.

"Sure, break me off a piece," Lucas said.

Aslan sat next to Kenny with drool coming out of both sides of his mouth. Apparently, the dog wanted a piece as well. Lucas wasn't sure that would be a good idea. He wasn't sure if dogs should have cupcakes. And especially not chocolate.

After eating the small piece Kenny handed over, Lucas reached for one of the dismissed snacks. "Let's open this bag of popcorn. I think dogs can have popcorn, right?"

Aslan scrambled to Lucas's side as he opened the bag and dropped a couple of popcorn kernels on the floor. Aslan gobbled them up.

Lucas turned on his desk computer, intending to find out who resided at the address from the manila envelope.

Aslan backed up and spun in a circle with his tail high and his ears back. He let out a series of frantic high-pitched barks that Lucas had never heard from the dog before. Was Kenny having another epileptic attack?

Jolted, Lucas assessed Kenny. But the boy seemed perfectly fine and as confused by Aslan's behavior as Lucas.

A strange smell drifted past Lucas's nose.

Sulfur?

Panic jackknifed through Lucas. Something was very wrong.

"Why must I go over this again?" Paige said. She'd relayed to Agent McIntosh and Special Agent in Charge Fritz Von Amici the events of the night of Donald Lessing's murder three times already. Not to mention the times before when she'd met with Agent McIntosh in Florida.

And each time she told her story, they asked questions that made her think they were deliberately trying to trip her up as if, somehow, she was remembering wrong. Anger burned low in her gut. She tried to keep this interrogation in perspective. They wanted to make sure she was solid on her testimony. She'd seen Donald deploy the tactic a time or two.

A sudden awful scent filled the office. She wrinkled her nose and clapped a hand over her mouth. "What is that?"

Both men made faces and fanned the air.

"Smells like rotten eggs," Agent McIntosh exclaimed.

"Gas!" Special Agent in Charge Von Amici jumped from his seat so fast the chair toppled over. "We have to get out of here."

Paige rose, already confused and dizzy from the smell filling her head.

Placing her hands on the table, she retched.

Agent McIntosh and Special Agent in Charge Von Amici flanked her, each grabbing an arm and tugging her out of the office and down the hallway toward an exit sign.

She dug in her heels and tried to break their hold. "My son. I have to get my son."

The two men tightened their grip on her, dragging her out the marked exit door into a stairwell. Something, besides the smell of gas, was very wrong.

ELEVEN

Lucas stuffed the file back into Paige's satchel, threw the strap over his shoulder and snagged Kenny around the waist while he held Aslan's leash in his other hand. The smell invading the Marshals office made his eyes water and nose burn. "We have to evacuate."

"The snacks!" Kenny struggled to get free.

"We'll buy more." Lucas carried him through the office toward the conference room where Paige was interviewing with the FBI agents.

The room was empty.

Panic flushed through Lucas's system. Where was Paige and the two agents?

Sera rushed up to them. "I'll take Kenny."

Brian reached them, too. "I've got Aslan." He reached for the leash and snagged it from Lucas's hand.

Grateful to his friends and colleagues, Lucas said, "Get them to safety."

Secure that Sera and Brian would protect the boy and dog by taking them out through the front exit, Lucas rushed to the parking garage stairwell. It made the most sense that the agents would take Paige out of the building through the closest exit. The disgusting scent of sulfur filling the building made bile rise in Lucas's throat.

Lucas pushed open the door of the stairwell. The odor

was strong, wafting up the flights of stairs. A heavy fog hung in the air. This wasn't an accidental gas leak.

Deep in his gut, Lucas was certain the smoke and odor were a ploy perpetrated by Colin Richter. The FBI agents were walking into a trap and putting Paige in the line of fire.

"You have to trust the deputies will keep Kenny safe."

Agent McIntosh's voice sounded breathless as Paige struggled to break free from the FBI agents' hold on her arms.

She trusted Lucas. She did. But she hated being separated from her son.

The smell of gas intensified. The stairwell reeked and a foggy smoke stung her eyes. This wasn't a normal natural gas leak. Her stomach recoiled with the realization that someone had used a smoke bomb–type device with the intent of flushing her out.

They pushed through the exit door into the fresh air of the parking garage.

She heard the beep of a car alarm disengaging and the flashing of lights on a black SUV up ahead. Their intent was clear. They planned to spirit her away from the scene. And she wasn't having it.

"No way," Paige said, putting all her weight onto her heels, forcing them to drag her forward. "I'm not leaving without my son."

The screech of tires on the concrete floor sent a sharp knife of fear stabbing through her spine. A dark blue sedan rounded the corner and came to an abrupt halt a few feet from where she struggled with the agents. The passenger-side door flung open, and Colin Richter stepped out with a gun aimed at her chest.

Agent McIntosh released her and grabbed for his weapon.

Special Agent in Charge Von Amici tucked her behind him and held up a hand. Dread gripped her by the throat. She wanted to scream but could barely take a breath.

"Stand down," Von Amici demanded of McIntosh. "Richter, this isn't a good plan. You don't want to do this."

Colin's laugh echoed off the concrete walls, a horrid sound that shuddered through Paige.

"Of course, I do, Special Agent in Charge Von Amici," Colin retorted in a mocking tone. "Give me the woman and you can walk."

"Boss, don't," McIntosh said, still aiming his weapon at Richter.

"Let's be reasonable," Von Amici said.

Another man stepped out of the sedan, also holding a nasty-looking weapon.

"Tsk-tsk," Colin said. "Unless you want to die, send the woman to me. She'll disappear and no one will be the wiser."

The scrape of a shoe on the concrete sent a fresh wave of fear through Paige as another of Colin's men stepped out from between two cars. Von Amici and McIntosh swiveled, facing the new threat, leaving Paige exposed. If she ran, she'd be mowed down. But standing in place wasn't an option.

She spun and sprinted toward the stairwell.

Colin took advantage of the FBI agents' distraction and rushed forward to grab ahold of Paige's wrist, pulling her up short and dragging her toward his vehicle.

"No!" she screamed.

Lord, please, help me!

Lucas burst out into the parking garage with his weapon at the ready and cataloged what was happening.

The FBI agents were being held at gunpoint and Colin was dragging Paige to a car.

Lucas's stomach dropped. He aimed at Colin, but the man pivoted, pulling Paige in front of him like a shield.

"Let her go," Lucas shouted.

McIntosh took advantage of the moment and tackled the bad guy standing between him and Lucas.

Special Agent in Charge Von Amici drew his weapon and aimed at Colin's henchmen on the other side of the sedan. "Drop your weapon."

Lucas noted Brian and Gavin moving stealthily through the garage toward them with their weapons drawn. No doubt Sera had Kenny and Aslan somewhere safe.

"You're surrounded," Lucas told Colin. "There's no way out of this for you. Let the woman go and put down your weapons."

Colin's only response was a wicked smile as he brought his weapon up to Paige's temple.

The cold metal pressed against her temple caused shivers of fright to wreck Paige's composure. She met Lucas's gaze. Where was Kenny? Was he safe? She had to believe Lucas wouldn't be here if he hadn't secured her son first. Lucas had grown fond of Kenny, just as she and Kenny had grown fond of Lucas.

She slanted a glance at the man holding her hostage. She could see that Colin did not have his finger on the trigger. But that didn't mean he couldn't or wouldn't shoot her. Why he hadn't already killed her, she didn't know. Maybe his boss wanted to do the honors himself. Or maybe he wasn't as sure of himself as he appeared. Lucas had said they were surrounded. She believed him.

"We found the file on Adam Wayne," she said to Colin,

hoping to create an opportunity for escape. "He's going to prison."

"He's not my concern," Colin retorted, pressing the gun harder to her temple.

Paige wasn't going to go quietly. She had a lot to live for. Her son and a future. She stared at Lucas, her heart filling with emotions she couldn't fathom or sift through at the moment. She had to break free of Colin.

She hoped to convey her intent to Lucas as she mouthed, *Shoot him.*

Lucas's gaze narrowed. He subtly shook his head.

Exasperated, she realized why he refused. She was in the way. Without giving herself time to chicken out, she slammed her elbow back into Colin's rib cage while at the same time stomping down hard on his instep. Colin grunted and loosened his hold, the weapon drifting away from her temple.

She dropped to the ground.

Gunfire erupted around her.

Colin dove into the sedan along with the driver, who hit the gas.

Paige turned her head in time to see Gavin and Brian jumping out of the way as the sedan sped out of the parking garage.

Then Lucas was there, gathering her close, "Are you okay?"

She clung to him. Her heart hammering frantically in her chest. Love detonated behind her rib cage. Her mind couldn't comprehend the realization. "I am now. Kenny?"

"He's safe with Sera," Brian said, as he and Gavin joined them where she and Lucas sat on the garage floor.

Agent McIntosh had Colin's man handcuffed a few feet away.

"That's it," Special Agent in Charge Von Amici spat out. "We are taking Mrs. Walsh into our protective custody."

A fresh jolt of panic revved through Paige's system. She grabbed handfuls of Lucas's shirt. "Please, don't let them take me."

"I won't," Lucas murmured for her ears only.

He wasn't about to let anyone, or anything, separate him from Paige again. He helped her to her feet, keeping an arm around her waist. Slipping the satchel off his shoulder and onto hers, he tucked her close to his side as the local police flooded the garage. After giving statements and being assured a BOLO—be on the lookout—for the sedan would be issued, officers led the felon, who'd immediately asked for a lawyer, away.

"Mrs. Walsh is coming with us," Von Amici stated in a grim tone.

Paige made a noise of distress in her throat and pressed closer to Lucas's side. Before Lucas could voice a protest, his boss spoke.

"Mrs. Walsh is on her way to a safe location," Gavin said in a tone that rivaled Von Amici's. "We will be relocating her into the program within the next day or so."

He turned to Lucas and Brian. "Get them to the ranch."

Gavin gestured to the stairwell door. "The emergency ventilation system has sucked up all the nasty odor of the smoke bomb." Addressing the two FBI agents, he said, "Do you want the recording of your witness interview?"

Shooting daggers with his eyes at Lucas and Paige, Von Amici turned and followed Gavin to the stairwell door.

McIntosh hesitated. "Maybe I should go with you as an extra set of hands to protect the witness?"

"Not necessary," Lucas said. "Who did you tell you were interviewing Paige here?"

"I didn't tell anyone. My boss and your boss made the arrangements," McIntosh said. "Von Amici is as motivated as I am to put Richter, and Wayne, behind bars."

With that, McIntosh headed to the stairwell entrance and disappeared inside the building.

Lucas's gut churned with apprehension. McIntosh sounded sincere. Lucas didn't exactly trust Special Agent in Charge Von Amici. The man was arrogant and a control freak. But there was no reason Lucas should think either of the FBI agents were in league with Colin Richter, Adam Wayne or Eliza Mendez. Yet, James's words about a leak replayed through Lucas's mind. Someone had supplied Colin with the information of where Paige would be.

"Mommy!"

Paige broke from Lucas's hold.

Kenny, Sera and Aslan hurried into the parking garage from the main entrance. Aslan's tail wagged. The dog didn't seem fazed.

Paige ran to Kenny and knelt down to examine the boy. "Are you light-headed? Feeling pins and needles? Is there an aura?"

Shaking his head, Kenny touched her face. "I'm not having a seizure, Mommy."

Paige hugged him close. "I was so scared."

"You're safe, Mama," Kenny patted her on the back. Tenderness filled Lucas and it took every ounce of resistance not to join in the hug. He cleared his throat. "Let's load up. The quicker we get to Camp Strong the better."

"What about my snacks?" Kenny complained as his mother picked him up into her arms.

"I'll get you more snacks," Lucas promised him as they all hustled to Brian and Sera's SUV.

Lucas secured Aslan in the back compartment and Kenny and Paige into the back seat. He decided to hop in next to Paige to let Sera ride in the front with Brian at the wheel. Keeping Paige close was his top priority.

Paige held Kenny close to her in the back seat of the SUV. Her heart rate beat too fast still and the tightness in her chest constricted her breathing.

Kenny squirmed to be free. "Mama, too tight."

Reluctantly, she released her hold on him as the SUV surged into the late morning traffic of San Antonio's downtown district. Brian drove and Sera sat in the front passenger seat.

Seated beside Paige, Lucas grasped her hands and curled his fingers around hers. "You're both safe now."

She tightened her hold on him. Yes, they were safe. But for how long? Would this nightmare ever end?

They were headed to a ranch outside of San Antonio, a waypoint on their way to being relocated into witness protection. Emotion clogged her throat, but she swallowed hard, keeping tight control of herself. She would not break down in front of these people.

"You promised we could stop at a store on the way to the ranch," she said to Lucas. "We still need supplies."

From the front passenger seat, Sera twisted to address her. "The Armstrongs will have everything you need. Toothbrushes, toothpaste, shampoo."

As much as Paige would appreciate all the toiletries, she was more concerned about clothing to get them started. Just a few items. "That's great to know. But Kenny and I have only the clothes on our backs. Plus, I really need to see if I can get more of his prescription."

Lucas sat forward to address his colleagues. "We can make a pit stop. We'll be quick about it."

"You don't think the assassin is following us, do you?" Paige asked.

"I've been keeping an eye out for a tail," Brian said from the driver's seat. "So far, so good."

"He has no idea where we're going, right?" Paige prompted.

"None," Sera agreed. "I don't think stopping will be a problem."

They left the hustle and bustle of the city limits behind as they headed through a suburb. Brian turned into a large strip mall parking lot where a multipurpose department store stood as the crowning jewel.

Brian brought the SUV to a halt in a parking spot underneath the shade of a tree planted in a green space with a nice strip of lawn. "I'll stay with the dog."

"Kenny and I will stay with Brian and the dog," Sera said, her gaze bouncing between Paige and Lucas.

"Let's make this quick." Lucas popped open his door and stepped out of the vehicle. He stood for a moment, blocking her from exiting the vehicle. Then he turned and offered her his hand. The kind gesture had affection unfurling in her chest and easing some of the tautness. She slipped her smaller hand into his large one. Their palms met. A sense of calm infused her at the contact. She climbed out and stood next to him.

"Don't forget the snacks," Kenny called after them.

"I wouldn't dream of it." Lucas grinned at her son and gave him a thumbs-up gesture.

Lucas put his hand on the small of Paige's back, creating a delightful kind of tension racing up her spine.

They hurried through the parking lot into the store. The swoosh of the doors closing behind them was a familiar and welcoming sound. Still, she needed this to be quick because she wanted to get back to her son. She headed directly to the pharmacy and made the request for a refill. While they waited, they headed to boy's department where she grabbed several essential items in Kenny's size and put them in the cart.

As Lucas escorted her toward the women's department, a sudden shyness gripped her. She paused mid-stride. "Maybe you should go get those snacks you promised."

For a moment, she thought he would argue. Then he glanced around, obviously looking for a threat. When his gaze came back to hers, she could see indecision warring in those deep brown eyes.

She put a hand on his arm. "I will be fine for the five minutes it takes you to grab some snacks."

He gritted his teeth. Once again, his gaze searched the area. "If you feel even the slightest twinge of unease, you scream and I'll come running."

His care and concern made tears prickle her eyes again. She blinked rapidly to hold them back. "Not a problem. I'll shatter the windows with my scream."

His mouth crooked upward at the corners. "That would be a feat."

"It won't be necessary," she said, hoping to be the one reassuring him this time.

He gave a quick nod and strode away. She watched him for a moment, marveling at how much she'd come to care and rely on this man. Silly of her when she knew she would be disappearing from his life soon.

She ducked into the women's department, blinking back fresh tears. Through a blurry haze, she grabbed a few necessary items and stuck them into her cart. On a whim, she grabbed a dress that looked feminine and flowy, along with a pair of strappy sandals. It was an indulgence she really didn't need but retail therapy was a much-appreciated soother.

She'd just reached the main aisle when Lucas came striding back, one arm filled with all sorts of snacks while the other hand carried a baseball mitt with a softball tucked inside.

He dumped the snacks into the cart but held on to the baseball mitt.

She stared at his hand and realized there were two mitts. One adult size and one child size.

For a moment, her world tilted, and she felt like she might topple over by the sudden flood of tenderness filling her veins and short-circuiting her brain.

"I hope it's okay," Lucas said obviously misreading her hesitation. "I thought Kenny and I could play catch at the ranch. But if you'd rather I didn't—"

Lucas was buying baseball equipment. For him and Kenny. Paige burst into tears.

"Hey, now," Lucas set the mitts and ball in the cart. Then he stepped close, his arms gently encircling her and drawing her to his chest.

She flung her arms around his waist, pressing her cheek against his beating heart. "That's the nicest thing anyone has ever done for us."

Lucas tightened his hold on her. She felt his kiss on her temple. She tilted her head up, meeting his gaze. Then his lips descended, capturing hers in a toe-curling kiss that chased away her tears and filled her with delight.

The clearing of a throat jolted them apart. Lucas kept an arm around her waist while his other hand rested on his sidearm.

An older couple smiled at them.

"Remember the days when we were like that?" the older gentleman said to his wife.

"What are you talking about? We're still like that!" the older woman said and drew her husband in for a quick kiss.

Paige couldn't help it. She burst into laughter. Lucas's chuckle warmed her heart.

The older gentleman winked. "Keep the romance alive and you'll end up celebrating a sixtieth anniversary like we are."

Paige stepped away from Lucas with a protest on her lips. But Lucas captured her hand, drawing her back to him and silencing her words.

"We will definitely keep that in mind," he said to the couple. "You two have a good day."

With that, Lucas pushed the cart with his free hand and tugged her along with him, leaving the older couple behind.

"Sixty years," Paige murmured. "Is that even possible?"

"Anything is possible," Lucas said. "Let's get that prescription so we can get out of here."

Paige tightened her hold on his hand and tucked away his words in her heart. They weren't a promise because he couldn't make that promise. But she would cherish them, anyway.

TWELVE

The SUV approached a metal arch with the words *Camp Strong* formed from the twisted and welded metal. Lush pastureland with grazing horses and an orchard with rows of trees stretched to the fence line. In the distance, a two-story craftsman-style house and other buildings came into view. Paige couldn't help but be impressed by the ranch.

"I wasn't sure what I was expecting, but this surpasses anything I could've imagined," she told Lucas.

They were seated in the back seat, with Kenny between them on the drive from San Antonio. The proximity made her achingly aware of him. Her gaze drifted to his mouth. Their kiss in the store replayed through her mind, a memory she would long savor. But neither of them had mentioned the kiss. In fact, Lucas has barely looked her way. Instead, he seemed to be keeping a vigil out the windows, constantly on alert for a threat.

As Brian slowed the vehicle, Kenny scrambled over her lap to stare out the window. Aslan roused from where he'd been sleeping in the back.

"Mama, can we pet the horses?"

"I'm sure that can be arranged," Lucas answered.

Paige slanted him a glance, not upset that he answered for her but more curious as to why he had. Did he think she'd say no? Or was it a habit for him to take charge? It probably hadn't occurred to him he was overstepping.

"We'll see what Mrs. Armstrong says about the horses," Paige told Kenny.

Lucas's questioning gaze captured and held Paige's. "She won't mind."

"Perhaps not, but we should ask the host before making promises," Paige said. "Don't you think?"

A lopsided grin appeared on Lucas's handsome face. "You're right. My bad."

Paige returned the grin, liking that he hadn't taken offense.

Brian brought the SUV to a halt at a wrought iron gate connecting two sides of fencing and entered a code into an electric keypad. The gate rumbled open. They drove forward and Paige turned around to watch the gates closing behind them.

"Is that an electrified fence?" she asked.

"It is," Lucas said.

"And it also sounds an alarm to the house if anyone breaks the circuit," Sera supplied from the front passenger seat.

Paige was doubly impressed. No one could get on the property without sending out an alert. "How long will we be here?"

"A couple of days," Lucas told her. "Gavin will bring the paperwork that we didn't get a chance to sign in the office. We'll get the ball rolling on your new identities."

Her heart thumped. "When are *you* leaving?"

Lucas angled toward her and reached across the seat to grasp her hand. He subtly looked toward the front seats and his fellow marshals and then back at Paige. "I will stay until everything is set and you are relocated."

Once again, she took his words as a promise.

Brian stopped the SUV in front of a beautiful home. A

wraparound porch with rocking chairs and dormer windows gave the place a storybook feel. It was something straight out of a magazine. Beyond the house, smaller cabins formed a half circle around a large firepit with benches. There were a couple of barns and in the distance there were more horses grazing. It all was so picturesque and peaceful. Nothing bad could happen here.

A woman with long red hair pulled back into a braid that trailed over her shoulder walked out of the house and down the steps to greet them. She was petite, wearing jeans, a Western-style shirt in shades of red and well-worn cowboy boots. If not for the crinkles at the corners of her green eyes, Paige wouldn't have guessed the woman was old enough to be Mrs. Armstrong.

Lucas squeezed her hand. "Let me introduce you to Victoria. I think you'll like her."

Why was Paige so nervous? She wanted to leave a good impression on this woman who was opening her home and providing safety for her and Kenny. Did Victoria understand the danger they brought?

After letting Aslan out of the back compartment and putting him on a leash, Lucas came around the SUV and opened the back passenger door. Kenny hopped out but stayed close as Lucas held out his hand to Paige. She accepted his offer of help and climbed out of the vehicle into the bright June day.

At the front of the vehicle, she watched as Brian and Sera took turns hugging Victoria Armstrong. She said something and they all laughed. Brian and Sera hurried inside the house.

Swallowing back her flutter of anxiety, Paige plastered a smile on her face and squared her shoulders. She didn't need to impress anyone. Yet, deep down, she really hoped Victoria approved of her. Which was ridiculous. What did it matter? This was a temporary situation and she'd never see the woman again. Still… Lucas clearly held Victoria in high esteem and Paige wanted to be well-thought-of by her, too, even if Lucas wouldn't be in Paige's life much longer, either.

The warring going on inside Paige's brain was making her exhausted.

Lucas kept ahold of her hand and they moved together to meet Victoria.

Victoria's sharp gaze darted to their joined fingers and then up to Lucas, a definite question in her eyes. Lucas remained silent. She turned her gaze to Paige.

Paige swallowed at the kindness and welcome she saw in the green depths of the other woman's eyes.

"Paige, Gavin has spoken highly of you," Victoria said. She smiled at Kenny, who hid behind Paige's leg.

Victoria squatted down and tilted her head. "You must be Kenny. Do you like soft pretzels with cheese?"

Kenny nodded.

Victoria grinned, rose and held out her hand to Kenny. "Come along. We better get in there before Brian and Sera eat them all."

Kenny looked up at Paige, clearly waiting for her permission.

Love for her son crowded her chest. "Go on. It's okay."

Kenny skipped forward and grasped Victoria's hand.

Over her shoulder, Victoria said, "Lucas, show Paige around. And you can let the dog off leash. I'll save you each a pretzel." Then she and Kenny disappeared inside the house.

Lucas's low chuckle reverberated within Paige's chest. She slanted him a glance. "What's so funny?"

"Victoria obviously believes we need a moment alone," he stated.

Paige held up their joined hands. "This might have had something to do with her assumption?"

Instead of letting her go as she expected, he tightened his hold.

One corner of his mouth lifted. "Yes, that might have something to do with it."

Then he did release her so he could unhook the leash from Aslan's collar. The dog didn't move but stared at them with a question in his eyes.

"Be free." Lucas waved his hand.

She pointed to the lawn. "Grass."

Aslan took off at a happy lope toward a large patch of grass with a huge tree that provided shade.

"Let's take a walk," Lucas said.

Paige hesitated. "What about Aslan?"

"He'll be safe."

"What if he goes into the pasture where the horses are?"

"They're used to dogs," he said. "Adele, Brian's wife, has brought her Dalmatian here multiple times. He's not a herder but he likes to round them up, anyway."

Paige couldn't imagine it. "Is that safe?"

"The horses are well trained," Lucas assured her. "And I can guarantee Aslan won't get under their feet. He's a smart boy. Plus, I have a feeling he's not going to stray far from you or Kenny."

There was truth in his words, so she allowed Lucas to lead her toward the back of the house.

Pointing to the area of the cabins and firepit, he said, "From what I've been told, when Jace, their only child, left home, Victoria wanted to do something productive with the place," Lucas said. "She formed a nonprofit and hosts at-risk youth camps throughout the year. The campers learn to ride and care for the horses as well as other life skills."

"Good for her." Paige wondered what she'd do when

Kenny left home. Where would they be? Who would they be? The questions burned holes through her mind.

True to Lucas's prediction, Aslan trailed close behind them until they were ready to go inside. The wraparound porch in the back almost mirrored the front. More rocking chairs lined the porch. Paige could envision warm nights sitting out with a glass of iced tea, watching the sunset, or in the morning holding a mug of coffee and watching the sunrise. She wasn't quite sure which direction the house faced or the path of the sun but the view would be spectacular regardless.

They entered the Armstrong home through the back door. The inside was as lovely as the outside. Gleaming cherrywood floors and Western-style furniture appeared comfy but upscale. The kitchen was impressive. A large island with a quartz countertop in white with a silver vein added a touch of whimsy in the middle of the room. A row of barstools provided seating at the island. A stainless-steel dishwasher and a double farm-style sink sat beneath a large window framed by pretty silver-and-white curtains. The cabinets were painted in a soft dove gray. A round table and chairs sat in a nook flanked by more windows, allowing lots of sunlight to stream into the house.

Seated at the table, Kenny, Sera and Brian were eating what looked like homemade soft pretzels, dipping cheese and an assortment of mustards.

Paige's stomach growled.

Victoria brought a fresh pitcher of lemonade to the table and two glasses and set them side by side at two empty chairs.

"As promised, we saved you some pretzels," Victoria said.

"Brian nearly ate them all," Sera teased as she scooped

a glop of cheese onto a piece of pretzel and popped it into her mouth.

Brian rubbed his belly. "Three was plenty."

Kenny giggled and tore off a chunk of the pretzel in front of him. "This is only my second one, Mama."

Lucas held out the seat next to Kenny and Paige sat. Lucas took the seat next to her. Victoria set a bowl of water on the floor. Aslan immediately lapped up the water and then moved to find a sunbeam to lie in.

Putting a pretzel on a plate, Paige said, "As afternoon snacks go, these are lovely. Thank you, Mrs. Armstrong."

With a wave, the older woman said, "Please, call me Victoria. Or Vicki. Or Vic. Or Tori. I'll answer to any of them."

Paige smiled, liking the woman. "Victoria it is, then."

"Paige, you and your son will be bunking upstairs. Along with Lucas. Brian and Sera will take cabins in the yard. I understand their spouses will be joining them later today."

Sera made a happy noise. "That's terrific. Thank you for inviting them."

"I figure we should just make it a party," Victoria said. "Jace and Abby will be flying in tomorrow."

"We'll have the whole gang here," Brian said, with pleasure dripping from his tone.

Sera turned to Paige. "Have we told you about the police academy? Brian, Jace and I went through it together."

Paige shook her head. "But I'd love to hear whatever stories you want to tell us."

Lucas rose from his seat, taking his plate with the pretzel and a large glob of cheese with him. He turned to Victoria. "I need to make a call. Do you mind if I use Gavin's office? Or would you prefer I go outside?"

"Either is fine with me," Victoria answered.

Lucas headed down the hallway and disappeared into a

room, shutting the door behind him and leaving Paige and Kenny with the other deputy marshals.

There was no reason for Paige to feel unsettled by his departure. He was within screaming distance. And she trusted Brian and Sera.

So why was her stomach in knots?

Gavin's office was dim. Lucas hesitated just inside the threshold after closing the door behind him. A large desk sat in front of a window with the curtains drawn closed. Onc wall had bookshelves and there was a game table with a jigsaw puzzle nearly done.

Lucas was uncomfortable invading his boss's private space.

It was strange having two bosses to answer to.

No.

Gavin was his boss now.

Not James. Still, Lucas felt loyalty to the Homeland Security agent and the now defunct task force that had brought Adam Wayne to justice.

For whatever reason, Lucas felt like he was betraying Gavin by calling James within the sanctity of Gavin's office. Nope, couldn't do it.

He eased open the door and quickly headed down the hallway to the side door that would take him out of the house. Hc had stayed here on numerous occasions over the past year and a half since he joined the San Antonio Marshals Service. Though he'd never stayed in the main house before, so that would be new. But from what he had gathered from his friends, being given a room in the house happened when a deputy brought someone to the ranch to protect.

It had worked out well for Jace and Abby, Brian and Adele. He wasn't sure if Sera and Duncan had stayed at the ranch. But it stood to reason they had. Sera certainly seemed comfortable here.

Being at the ranch made him miss his own family. What would his mother, sisters and father think of Paige and Kenny? Would they accept a ready-made family?

He groaned aloud. Stalking toward the lone tree in the yard, he shook his head at his own foolishness.

What was he doing thinking about his protectees that way?

Paige and Kenny were going into witness protection. End of story.

Stop fantasizing about a future that will not, cannot, happen.

Giving himself a mental head slap, he sat down on the grass, leaned back against the tree trunk and balanced his plate on his thighs. Using the cell phone he'd bought along the way, he dialed James's private number and waited for him to pick up

"Who's speaking?" James's voice came over the line.

"Cavendish here," Lucas said.

"Is the witness secure?" James barked out the question.

"She is, sir. But we had a mishap at the Marshals office in San Antonio."

"Yes, I heard," James replied, his voice hard. "The FBI has been tearing into me like dogs on fresh meat. They want to know where the witness is. The local authorities found the sedan Colin escaped in abandoned near the River Walk in downtown San Antonio," James stated. "Wayne and his lawyer are in the wind. I have people searching for them but I'm afraid they may have skipped the country."

Frustration beat behind Lucas's eyes. "We'll be relocating Paige and her son into witness protection within the next day or so. They will be out of harm's way."

Guilt and responsibility descended on Lucas's shoulders.

He'd done what he could. His mission had been to protect Paige and Kenny, which he'd accomplished. But they would never be free as long as Adam Wayne, Eliza Mendez and Colin Richter were at large.

"This is not going well. I need that file," James said. "I'll come to Texas to get it. I don't trust anyone else."

"I'll keep this phone on and be ready to meet you with the file when you arrive in town," Lucas told James.

A harrumph from the end of the other line was the only response Lucas got before the line went dead.

Lucas made his way back into the house, apprehension tightening his shoulder muscles. There was no reason for the unwarranted caution tripping up his spine. The circle of people aware of this location was small.

Paige glanced at his still uneaten pretzel on the plate in his hand. "Did the call not go well?"

Lucas set the plate on the kitchen table and picked up the glass of lemonade. "I lost my appetite."

He took a long pull from the lemonade, letting the tart and sweet liquid replenish his body and quench his thirst. But he wasn't sure what would calm his nerves.

"Let's get you all settled in your rooms," Victoria said. "I asked Brian and Sera to bring in whatever bags you have."

Lucas escorted Paige and Kenny to the bottom of the staircase where they found the bags of clothing from the big-box store. He picked them up and Victoria led the way up the stairs.

She opened a room and gestured. "Paige and Kenny, you'll share here. I had Gavin bring up one of the cots for Kenny."

"That was very thoughtful of you," Paige said as she, Kenny and Aslan entered the room.

Lucas was surprised by how feminine the room was in crisp blues and whites with fresh flowers in a vase on a bedside table. A pink cowboy hat sat on the bed. The image popped into his head of Paige wearing that hat, jeans and a fringed shirt like one of the rodeo princesses, and sitting on one of the ranch's big beautiful horses. Did she ride?

A question to be answered later. Or not at all. They weren't here for pleasure. His conversation with James had driven that truth home.

He backed out of the room and into the hall.

Victoria flashed him a smile before she opened the door of the room directly across from Paige and Kenny's. "This will be your room, Caveman."

Lucas winced. Of course, Victoria Armstrong would know his military call name. And probably the reason behind it. He just hoped Paige hadn't heard and wouldn't ask questions.

"I'll let you two get settled," Victoria said and turned her focus to Kenny. "Would you like to see the horses?"

Lucas dropped his chin and stared at the petite woman. Was she matchmaking?

The surprise on Paige's face morphed into tenderness and she nodded. "That's very nice of you to offer. Kenny, what do you say?"

"Yes, please!" The boy danced in place with excitement.

Victoria gave Lucas an innocent look as she took Kenny's hand and they practically skipped down the stairs and out the door with Aslan following close behind.

For a moment, neither he nor Paige moved, then she propped a shoulder against the door of her room. "Caveman? That's a story I'd like to hear."

Lucas gritted his teeth to hold back a groan of frustration. "One for another time."

Paige arched an eyebrow. "I'll hold you to that promise."

He hadn't meant for his words to sound like a promise. But for some reason, this woman got under the barriers around his heart. If he weren't careful, he'd fall in love with her. And that would be a disaster.

Time to retreat. "I'm going to freshen up."

He stepped back and shut the door, closing Paige out. Okay, that may have been cowardly. But he needed a moment to himself, to get his emotions under control. The last thing either of them needed was heartache on top of the danger lurking outside the fenced perimeter.

THIRTEEN

Paige stared at the closed door of Lucas's guest room. Well. Okay. He didn't want to talk to her about his past.

Nor did he want to acknowledge what Victoria was trying to do. An old Broadway tune from the musical *Fiddler on the Roof* played through her head.

Victoria wanted to play matchmaker.

Neither did she want to admit to Victoria's machinations, but still… Why did his rejection of the idea of them together sting?

Ridiculous of her to care.

She retreated into her appointed guest room and unpacked her and Kenny's recently purchased items. Her mind wandered to the kiss she and Lucas had shared. How firm his mouth had been, yet so gentle and coaxing. She'd liked the way his hand had cupped the back of her head.

"Stop it!" Saying the words aloud helped her to recenter her thoughts. Letting her mind wander to the attraction zinging between them wasn't productive. Despite how much she'd grown to care for Lucas, she had to remember this was all temporary.

A commotion filled with Aslan's barking outside her window had her rushing to lean over the desk, move aside the curtain and stare out. Gavin Armstrong had arrived, and Aslan was greeting him.

Gavin bent and rubbed the dog behind the ears.

Victoria and Kenny came out of the barn.

Paige's heart squeezed at the sight of the husband and wife embracing, then Victoria and Kenny went back into the barn while Gavin returned to his vehicle and grabbed what Paige guessed was the witness protection program paperwork she hadn't been able to sign back at the Marshals office.

With a sigh of resignation, she left the room, and just as Lucas disappeared down the stairs ahead of her. Her steps were slow as she made her way to where she heard the men talking.

"Once we get this taken care of," Gavin was saying, "the ball will move swiftly."

The ball, meaning her and Kenny's lives. She was thankful for Victoria keeping Kenny occupied.

This was going to be hard enough without having to explain the process to Kenny. She'd already told him that they would be given new identities when they moved to a new city.

Paige entered the kitchen to find Gavin had placed the paperwork on the dining table along with a thick binder.

Gavin smiled. "How are you holding up, Mrs. Walsh?"

Returning his smile was difficult. "Please, call me Paige." Her stomach knotted, knowing very soon she wouldn't answer to that name again.

"Please, take a seat," Gavin gestured to the nearest chair.

"Here, let me." Lucas moved swiftly to pull out the chair for her.

Smiling her gratitude at him came more naturally. "Thank you." She sat and put her hands on the kitchen table to brace herself as she faced the marshal. "Can we get this over with?"

Beside her, Lucas had taken a seat. He touched her elbow, drawing her attention. "Would you like some water?"

Touched by his thoughtfulness, she nodded. "Please."

Lucas rose and strode into the kitchen. Her gaze tracked him as he took a glass from the cupboard and filled it with water from the refrigerator door. He seemed comfortable here at the ranch. Everybody seemed comfortable at the ranch. She wished she could be as well.

But she would not get comfortable. She needed to build up the walls around her heart and live in reality. Soon this would all be a distant memory.

Taking the first step into her new world had to happen now. She looked at the marshal. "Where will we be going?"

"That will be determined after you fill out the paperwork." He put his hand on the binder. "Read through this carefully. Respond to all the questions. I will have an answer for you tomorrow morning."

She wrinkled her nose. "Is this some kind of test?"

"Of a sort," the marshal said. "We need to know as much as we can about you, your life and your past so that we make sure you don't intersect with anyone who could compromise you and your location."

Lucas returned to the seat beside her, setting down a glass of water. "Take your time. We don't have to finish this tonight."

But she did. She wanted this over with. She wanted to get to the next phase of her life. Because the longer she stayed here, the longer she was with Lucas, the harder leaving would be. She didn't want to admit it, but she was falling for the handsome deputy.

Taking a breath to clear her thoughts, she opened the binder and began to read, answering the questions as she went with the pen provided. Some were very superficial queries, such as where had she grown up. What street had she lived on? Who were her friends as a child, in adolescence and as a young adult? The names of the schools she'd attended, the churches and the organizations she belonged to.

But the questions grew harder, digging deeper into her life and her marriage, the further she read. Answering questions about her deceased husband's life created an ache of sadness. Not just for herself, but for Kenny, too. Everything about his father would be erased from their lives.

She paused at a question asking about any living relatives. Where did they reside? When was her last contact with them?

Her father was her only living relative. It had been several days since their last conversation and they were due for another call in a few days. How could she go the rest of her life not seeing him? He'd been her rock when Paul died. She'd watched him care for her mother with such love and tenderness as the cancer ate away at her.

Paige couldn't imagine a life where her father wasn't a part of it. A life where Kenny never had a chance to know his grandfather.

She couldn't do it. Regret that she hadn't followed her father to Germany sliced through her. She should have taken Kenny overseas by now. It had been a year and a half since she and Kenny had seen her father. Time missed when they could have been together.

She put down the pen. Her hand shook as she grasped the water glass and brought it to her lips. The cool liquid soothed her parched throat and raw nerves.

"We should take a break," Lucas said. "You've been at this for an hour."

"I can't go any further until I'm allowed to contact my father," she said, infusing steel into her voice. "I can't drop off the face of the earth without telling him. It's not fair. It would be cruel." She couldn't bear knowing he would be tormented if she and Kenny simply disappeared without any explanation. He would tear the world apart searching for them. He would never be at peace.

For a long moment, neither man spoke.

Lucas covered her hand with his. "It would be dangerous to contact him."

"How?" She curled her fingers around his and hung on. "Tell me how saying goodbye puts anyone in danger? I don't know where I'm going. I don't know what name we'll be living under. I can't reveal any information to him that would put me and Kenny at risk. You keep talking about danger, but I think we've already been through enough scares to know safety isn't a guarantee."

Gavin steepled his fingers, resting his elbows on the table. "We can get a message to him. If you want to write him a note."

She could see by the expression in his hard gaze that he would not budge. A letter to her father was the most they would give her.

She hated this. Why had she gone back to Donald's office? Why couldn't she have just mailed that manila envelope without worrying about whom it was supposed to be addressed?

Her stomach pitched and tears pricked the backs of her eyes. "Fine. If you don't mind, I'll retire to my room where I can write a note to my father in private."

She released Lucas's hand and stood, her chair scraping on the floor, the sound shuddering down her spine.

Gavin nodded and the sympathy in his gaze twisted her heart up like one of Victoria's homemade pretzels.

Lucas rose, placed his hand on the small of her back and escorted her up the stairs.

"Afraid I'll run away?" She couldn't keep the irritation from lacing her words.

"Of course not," he said, his voice soft and soothing. "I

just want to make sure you're all right. I know this is a lot. It's hard. But you'll get through it."

She turned and met his gaze. Did he really understand? No doubt he'd seen many people in this situation break down. She wasn't going to be one of them. At least not for him to witness. Straightening her spine, she lifted her chin. "Yes, I will get through this. As I get through everything in life, without relying on anyone else's help."

"Paige, please—"

She held up a hand, cutting him off. "Don't. You'll only make it worse. This is the way it has to be. We both know it."

He sighed and raked his fingers through his hair. "I've come to care for you and Kenny. More than I should."

"You'll forget about us in no time," she told him, fearing the truth in her words. But she wouldn't ever forget him. She stepped into the room Victoria had graciously loaned her. "I'll be down in a while."

She shut the door and leaned her back against the wood. "Dear Father in Heaven, I know You have a plan. A plan for good not evil in my life and in Kenny's. I trust You. I really do. But this is so hard. I just don't understand why this is happening to us."

On shaky legs, she headed to the desk where she'd earlier seen stationery paper and pens. Her stomach grumbled. It would be a while before dinner. She couldn't think on an empty stomach. She grabbed her satchel from where she'd dropped it on the bed and rummaged through it, looking for the protein bar she'd taken from the cabin. Her hand closed around another object. One she'd forgotten about.

The cell phone Lucas had bought her at the convenience store. The need to hear her father's voice overwhelmed her. She weighed the phone in her hand. It was a burner phone, unattached to her in any way. Weren't they designed to keep the caller anonymous? It was impossible anyone could trace the call back to her. And her father was so far away in Germany. There was no way the bad guys would be watching him and monitoring his phone.

She needed to hear her father's voice one last time before she and Kenny were whisked away to an unknown place with an unknown fate.

Would the burner make an international call? Only one way to find out. Thankfully, she had her father's number memorized. Not allowing herself to dwell on the fact that she was about to betray Lucas's trust, she punched in the country code for Germany and then the number. There was static, then a ringing tone as the call connected to her father's house phone. A flutter of anxiety started in the pit of her stomach and moved up into her chest as she waited. Was she making a mistake?

Lucas would be angry with her. Did she really want to break his trust?

Just as she was about to hang up, her father answered.

"Hello, who is this?" Her father deep voice brought fresh tears to her eyes. His American accent had been tainted by his time in Germany. Or rather his German accent had been tainted by his time in America and now had reverted back to his original accent.

"Papa, it's me," she said, keeping her voice low in case Lucas was still outside her door.

"Paige! Are you okay? I wasn't expecting you to call today."

How much should she tell him? Tears flowed freely down her cheeks. "Papa, I only have a moment. Something terrible has happened. My boss was murdered and I'm a witness. Kenny and I must disappear. I will reach out to you again as soon as I can."

"How could this happen? Where are you going? I'll be right there!"

"No, Papa. You can't come here. You can't tell anyone you heard from me. I'm breaking all kinds of rules by calling you. I just couldn't... I mean... Please, know that I love you. I will send word when I can." She hung up.

Guilt knifed through her, scoring her all the way to the quick. What had she just done?

She tossed the phone back into the satchel and sent up a prayer for forgiveness. But really it was Lucas she needed to ask forgiveness of. Her stomach clenched with dread. Breaking rules went against her very core beliefs. Yet, she couldn't really regret hearing her father's voice again or telling him she loved him.

She headed for the door but then stopped. She still wanted to write a letter to her father. She returned to the desk and sat down with the paper and pen. She poured out her heart to her father about her boss's murder and about her feelings for Lucas. When she was done, she slipped the letter into an envelope and sealed it. Holding it to her chest, she prayed that the Marshal Services wouldn't open the note before sending it.

The thought gave her pause. No way did she want anyone other than her father to read what she'd written about Lucas. She couldn't risk it.

She stuffed the letter in her satchel and started over. This time the letter was much more generic, giving her father basically the same information she'd given him on the phone. She folded the letter and put it into a new envelope, but this time didn't seal it just in case. She opened the door and was almost surprised to find the hall empty. Slowly, she returned to the kitchen dining area where Lucas sat alone at the table.

"Gavin had to take a call from the FBI," Lucas told her.

She handed him the note. She couldn't stop the tears from starting again. Lucas rose and engulfed her in his embrace. She laid her head against his chest, feeling the rhythmic beat of his heart against her cheek. She never wanted to leave him. But she had to. So indulging in this moment wouldn't harm anything, would it?

Lucas's heart raced and emotions clogged his throat. He'd seen witnesses break down before going into the program. It was a lot to take in. A lot to process. But this was the first time he'd felt this amount of empathy. His sisters would have a field day if they knew how deeply he'd fallen for this woman. But no one would know. He couldn't let on how he felt no matter how much he wanted to. Holding Paige in his arms tested his mettle and resolve like nothing else could.

Needing to distract Paige for both their sakes, Lucas said, "How about we go out and watch Kenny ride a horse?"

Paige sniffled and lifted her head. It took all of Lucas's strength of will not to kiss away the upset in her pretty eyes.

She stepped back and took a shuddering breath, wiping away the tears from her cheeks. "Thank you. I don't know why I am so emotional."

"It's totally understandable." Lucas grabbed his hat off the back of the kitchen chair and placed it on his head, then he held open the back door for Paige to walk out.

The sunshine bathed the world in a bright glow. Off to the left was a small corral where they could see Kenny astride a large beautiful brown horse. Victoria stood beside him with the reins in one hand while her free hand had ahold of Kenny's knee. She slowly walked the horse around the corral.

Lucas smiled at the sight. Somewhere, Victoria had

found a child-size cowboy hat to plop on Kenny's blond head to keep the sun from burning his scalp and face.

For a long moment, Paige stood watching. The tender emotion on her face nearly buckled Lucas's knees. Then she briskly walked forward until she came to the railing where she leaned her forearms against the top rail.

Lucas followed and stopped beside her, putting one foot on the bottom rail and his forearm on his knee. "Do you ride?"

"Not since I was a child," she told him. "There used to be a dairy farm near where I grew up that had horses. Every school year we would take a field trip there to learn about dairy farming and have a ride on a horse." She gave a small laugh. "Though, those horses were small and not nearly as beautiful as the one Kenny is riding."

The image of a young Paige on a small horse made Lucas smile. "You might've been riding a pony?"

"Probably," she said. "My parents weren't big on animals."

"No dog growing up? Cats?"

"Neither. My first experience with a dog has been Aslan."

Lucas's gaze sought the dog who lay in the shade of the barn, watching. He noticed Aslan's leash, though still attached to his collar, was not tethered to anything. "He's a good boy."

"That he is. A godsend." She tilted her head toward Lucas. "Before we had Kenny's seizures under control, Aslan was very busy. But now—"

"Now you have Kenny's epileptic episodes under control," Lucas finished for her. Something he was glad of. He'd witnessed one of the boy's seizures and knew how scary it must've been for Paige, especially before she knew what was causing them. He couldn't imagine the heartache of being a parent and not knowing how to help your child.

"It's quite a blessing that the one seizure he's had through all the stress was mild," Paige said.

"A testament to how calm you've been," Lucas said.

She faced him. "I attribute it to you."

Though her words flattered, he didn't feel he deserved them. He'd done nothing but his job.

A little more than your job, his conscience reminded him. He'd kissed his witness. Not once, but twice. And his heart was tangled up in her well-being.

Shaking off that disturbing thought, because, really, there was no place for emotion in the equation, he said, "We have a few hours before the others arrive. Would you like to try to ride a horse?"

Paige shook her head. "I'll let Kenny have the fun. I'm enjoying watching him. We'll both need a nap soon."

He couldn't fault her for declining. They weren't here on holiday. No matter how much he wished they were. The danger still lurked out there beyond the perimeter of the ranch fence, like a snake coiled and waiting to strike.

But Lucas would do everything in his power to ensure Paige and Kenny stepped into their new life without suffering any harm, including heartbreak.

He dismissed the pain his own heart would sustain when they had to say goodbye.

FOURTEEN

"Get a move on," Paige told Kenny after their afternoon nap. They'd both needed the rest. Kenny from the excitement of riding a horse and her from the emotional roller coaster of hearing her father's voice and the yo-yoing of her heart. One minute she wanted nothing more than to stay within Lucas's embrace and the next resigned to being without him for the rest of her life, which only made her sad and mad and...

She shook off the thoughts and took a calming breath. "I can smell something delicious cooking."

Kenny breathed in deeply. "Yum. Me, too. I'm hungry. Riding the range is hard work."

Paige pressed her lips together to keep a laugh from escaping. "I would imagine it is. Very serious business."

"Miss Victoria said tomorrow we can go out into the pasture," Kenny told her.

Paige refrained from responding. From the moment Kenny had dismounted off the horse, he'd been a bundle of joyous energy. He babbled about how much fun riding was, how great it was to be at the ranch and asked if he could have his own horse. Instead of bursting his bubble, she'd stayed quiet, letting him enjoy this time. Tomorrow would be soon enough to tell him they were leaving the ranch and no, a horse most likely wasn't in their future.

Though, why Victoria had made such a promise about tomorrow, Paige didn't know. Surely, the woman knew they would be relocated soon. When Gavin had left with the signed paperwork, he had told her to be packed and ready in the morning to leave. She let out a silent sigh filled with sad distress. She didn't relish the scene Kenny would make when it was time to go. Or the anguish they'd both feel to say goodbye to Lucas.

After putting on his shoes, Kenny grabbed the small cowboy hat and put it on his head. "I'm all ready."

Paige's gaze snaked to the pink cowboy hat she'd set on the desk. The temptation to put it on was strong but she resisted. No cute accoutrement was going to ease the sorrow already burrowing deep inside her heart. She hustled Kenny and Aslan downstairs and found two new people had joined them during her and Kenny's nap.

The tall dark-haired handsome man who sat on a barstool had to be Sera's husband. While the pretty blonde, wearing an elegant pantsuit, held hands with Brian. Undoubtedly his wife.

Lucas rose from the table and made the introductions.

Paige shook hands with DEA Agent Duncan O'Brien and then with Judge Adele Weston-Forrester.

Kenny tugged on Lucas's shirtsleeve. "When do we eat?"

"Kenny, that's rude," Paige chided.

"Sorry, Mama." Kenny tucked his hands behind his back.

"Let's go on out and see what the marshal has for us," Lucas said, leading the procession out the back door with Kenny following right on his heels and Aslan right behind Kenny.

Paige hurried to follow her family. The thought sent a pang of longing and despair arrowing through her.

Tables had been set up near the firepit. Victoria and Gavin had readied a barbecue nearby. There was another table piled high with bowls of fruit, potato salad and green salad. A plate stacked with brownies was close to the edge, placed just right for small hands to grab. Kenny snagged one and popped it into his mouth before Paige could shoo him away. Everyone laughed.

Lucas also took a brownie and ate it with gusto.

Paige's heart squeezed tight.

Over the next two hours, despite telling herself to keep her distance, Paige laughed so much more than she had in years. They played games, sang campfire songs and told stories of past adventures. Hearing how Adele and Brian met and fell in love had Paige on the edge of her seat. Like her, Adele had needed the deputy marshal to protect her from harm after her courtroom was blown up and they'd had to hide together. Their story had turned out well.

Then hearing Duncan and Sera explain how going undercover as Santa and Mrs. Claus had turned into a deadly fight for their lives had Paige's nervous system firing. She was happy they'd had a good outcome.

Lucas sat beside her with a sleepy Kenny on his lap.

Paige wanted the night to never end. She liked all of these people. But she didn't belong. She only belonged with Kenny.

Would she find a community for her and Kenny in their new life? A group of people who loved her son and accepted her into their group with such ease?

Afraid she might start weeping again, Paige whispered to Lucas, "We should call it a night."

"I'll carry him," Lucas offered.

Grateful, Paige smiled her thanks. And she didn't miss the speculating glances between his colleagues and their spouses.

Her cheeks heated but she held her head high and led the way to the house. Aslan stayed close to Lucas. The house was softly lit as they went up the stairs to the room she and Kenny shared. Lucas gently laid Kenny on the cot. Paige quickly divested Kenny of his shoes and jeans, letting him sleep in his T-shirt.

Without protest, Kenny snuggled into the covers. Paige figured one night of not brushing his teeth wouldn't hurt him. Aslan lay on the floor, flopping onto his side with a soft noise that Paige decided was contentment.

A sentiment she wished she could share but with an uncertain future looming ahead, her mind and heart were filled with angst.

She walked Lucas to the door. "Thank you, again."

He gave her a crooked smile that set her heart fluttering in her chest.

"I'll be just across the hall after I help clean up," he said, keeping his voice low.

"Oh, I should help, too," she said, not wanting to be an ungrateful guest.

"I'm sure Victoria would appreciate the thought, but she'd be the first to tell you guests don't have to clean up."

Paige narrowed her gaze. "But aren't you a guest? And the others?"

"Technically. But not really," he told her. "The boss has us out here often. Team building. It took me a while to acclimate. Bonding isn't really my thing."

"I don't believe that," she said. "You've bonded with us." The words were out before she'd thought to stop them.

"You're special," he murmured.

As much as she wanted to hear those words from him, she couldn't let them go down this road. "It's wonderful you have a circle of friends and colleagues who have your back no matter what."

"You'll have the same one day," he told her.

She wanted to believe him. But doubt taunted her. Would

she ever allow anyone close again? Probably not. "It's a nice thought. Good night, Lucas."

Lucas dipped his chin and stepped out of the room. After readying herself for bed, she lay between the crisp sheets, listening to the soft breathing of her son and Aslan while the ambient light sneaked around the curtains, lulling her to sleep.

Several hours later, a high-pitched noise jackknifed Paige's heart and she jumped out of bed.

"Mommy?" Kenny's scared voice came at her in the dark from where he'd slept on the cot provided by Victoria.

Paige rushed to her son's side as he rose from the cot. Aslan panted and paced, a clear sign he was upset by the shrieking sound tearing through the house. Not a smoke alarm. A security system alarm.

Someone had breached the perimeter of the property.

Paige gathered Kenny close and grabbed ahold of Aslan's collar. Panic raced along her limbs, making her body shake. What was happening? How close was the danger? She needed to find Lucas.

She pushed Kenny and Aslan into the bathroom. "Stay in here. Don't come out unless it's me or Lucas."

"Mommy, you can't go!" Kenny said. "It's dangerous. Lucas said there were bad men after us. You have to stay with me."

Paige knelt and took his sweet little face in her hands. "I will be right back. I just need to check in with Lucas. He may want us to leave. But I won't expose you until I know what's happening. Please understand."

Kenny's body shook beneath her fingers. She released him and hustled to her satchel where she grabbed his rescue medication. It might be a bit premature, but she felt the alarm would induce a seizure. The doctor told her the earlier they could catch the seizures the better. She popped out one of the pills from the foil tab. "Put this under your tongue, sweetheart," she told him.

Kenny quickly did as she asked.

"Now get in the bathtub, please," she told him thinking that was the safest hiding place.

Paige quickly eased out of the bathroom and shut the door. She was thankful there was a small window that provided illumination from the outside security lights into the bathroom. Kenny and Aslan wouldn't be in darkness and their presence wouldn't be given away by turning on the bathroom light.

Paige hurried out of the bedroom and ran into Lucas.

He grasped her by the biceps. "Where's Kenny?"

"Hiding in the bathtub. Are we under siege?"

"Possibly," he said, propelling her back into the bedroom. "Grab the file." He released his hold on her. "I'll get Kenny and Aslan."

"Where are we going?"

Over his shoulder, he said, "To a safe room."

Of course, the Armstrongs would have a safe room. Paige was grateful to be in such a secure place. She grabbed her satchel with the Wayne file and Kenny's medicine. Then she stuffed a few garments for both her and Kenny inside. She was becoming used to preparing for just about anything. Lucas carried Kenny out of the bathroom. Aslan stayed close by his side.

They hurried down the staircase and into the living room where Gavin and Victoria waited for them.

Lucas set Kenny on his feet. Paige took ahold of his hand. "Stay close."

"We need to secure the judge," Gavin said as he handed Lucas a large rifle. "We'll get the civilians into the bunker and then we'll check the fence line."

Paige noticed that Victoria held a handgun at her side as they left the house. Outside, they met up with Sera and Duncan, both wearing tactical gear with night vision goggles hanging around their necks. Paige had never used the spy-like equipment, but she'd seen them on television enough to recognize the special eyewear. Her heart thumped. This was surreal.

Brian and Adele hurried from one of the cabins.

"This way," Gavin said, leading them to the horse barn.

Once inside, Gavin and Victoria opened the stall doors and ushered the horses out the back of the barn, setting them loose into the pasture. Gavin ducked into one of the open stalls.

"Will the horses be okay?" Kenny asked, his voice rife with worry.

"They're smart animals," Lucas told Kenny. "They will be fine."

"It will be a treat for them to be out at night," Victoria assured Kenny.

Paige gave the woman a grateful smile before saying, "I thought we were headed into a safe room."

"We are," the older woman said. "This way."

Surprised to see Victoria disappear into the same horse stall Gavin had gone into, Paige turned to Lucas. "What's happening?"

"They built a bunker under the barn for emergencies," he told her.

Brian and Adele hurried into the horse stall. Lucas gestured for Paige to follow. Holding Kenny's hand, Paige moved into the horse stall. Aslan panted by her side.

The hay covering the floor had been swept aside and a trapdoor in the ground was open.

Brian kissed his wife before she climbed down a ladder into the darkness below. Victoria turned on a light somewhere in the space, illuminating the ladder.

"Paige, please go," Lucas urged, putting his hand on her arm.

"Not without you," she said. "If this is The Beast, then you're in as much danger as I am. We have to stick together."

"I need to confront this threat," Lucas said, his voice hard. "I need to end this once and for all."

"At the risk to yourself?" She shook off his hand and stepped back. "You're willing to be reckless with your own life."

"This is what I am trained for," he said.

His words didn't ease any of her anxiety or simmering anger. Her deceased husband had been reckless and thought he was invincible.

Everything inside Paige rebelled. She didn't want to let Lucas go. She understood that this was his job. That every day was dangerous for him and the other marshals. But it didn't sit well that he could be walking straight into the line of fire, knowing he was just as much of a target.

He helped Kenny down the ladder, then with Gavin's help lowered a very patient Aslan into the bunker.

"Your turn," Lucas said, holding out his hand. "Every moment counts."

Sensing the urgency in his tone, she moved to the ladder. An awful thought marched across her mind, weakening her knees. She hung on to Lucas. "There's something I need to tell you."

He touched her cheek. "Save it for later." He stepped back. "In you go."

"Come on, Mommy." Kenny urged from below.

"Paige, let Lucas do his job," Victoria said in a firm voice.

Pressure built in Paige's chest. She hurried down the ladder. The trapdoor was lowered above her, closing with a sharp click.

Paige made a sound of distress deep in her throat as the

horror of what she'd done cascaded over her like a bucket of ice water.

This was her fault. She'd brought this on them. She'd called her father. Somehow the bad guys had been watching him. Monitoring his phone. But how had they traced the burner phone? She thought such a thing was impossible. But what did she know about tracing calls or tracking down people? Nothing. Nothing at all. And she'd put everyone here at the ranch in danger because of her own selfish need to assure her father that she and Kenny were alive. She should have heeded Lucas's warning.

Please, God, forgive me.

Would Lucas forgive her?

Guilt-ridden, she allowed Victoria to tug her deeper into the underground bunker. It was bigger than she'd have imagined, running approximately the length of the horse barn. Concrete and steel walls held several cots as well as a pantry of shelves filled with food and water that could last a very long time. Adele paced.

Kenny sat on a cot with his knees drawn to his chest. Paige hurried to sit beside him and gathered him close. Aslan hopped up next to them and lay down, with his head on Kenny's knee.

"It's okay, Mommy," Kenny said, his arms going around her neck. He pressed his cheek to her shoulder. "The cowboy will keep us safe."

But who would keep him safe? Paige lifted a prayer asking, pleading with, God to spare all their lives. To spare Lucas.

Panic crawled through Lucas's bloodstream like fire ants as he hustled to the driveway in front of the Armstrongs' house where Brian, Sera, Duncan and Gavin had gathered.

Someone—no doubt Colin—had infiltrated the ranch's security perimeter. How had he known where they were?

Only a small handful of people were privy to this location. Lucas trusted all of them with his life.

His heart hiccuped as he thought about Paige and the way she had pleaded with him to stay, wanting him to be safe. Her words that she had something to tell him had sent a sliver of a different kind of panic arrowing into his heart. Had she foolishly gone and fallen in love with him?

No. He couldn't believe that. They had barely spent any time together.

But deep inside, he knew she could've fallen for him just as he had fallen for her.

He loved her. The thought rocked him back on his heels.

But there was nothing either of them could do about it. And right now, his focus had to stay razor-sharp or the consequences could mean death. Death for himself. His team members. Paige and Kenny.

He hadn't lied to Paige. He was going to confront Colin and somehow, someway, bring an end to the threat hanging over Paige.

"We have to find where the breaches are and plug the holes," Gavin said. "Duncan, Sera and Brian, you go along the fence line to the right. Lucas and I will go left."

After checking their weapons, the group dispersed.

"It's a lot of ground to cover," Lucas said. "We need more bodies here."

"The cavalry will arrive soon," Gavin told him. "The alarm silently alerts the US Marshals Service and SAPD."

Lucas was impressed. But keeping his wife and family safe with such measures must help Gavin sleep at night. Lucas knew it would take something similar for him to be able to ever— He cut off the thought.

If he ever married, he could only imagine himself with

one particular woman. And the only way that would ever happen was if he somehow managed to neutralize the danger to her life.

Lucas and Gavin hustled along the fence line looking for where the break was and keeping alert to any of Colin's men who might have gained access to the ranch.

A faint familiar noise that was incongruent with the topography raised the hairs on the back of Lucas's neck. Then he lost the sound as the wail of sirens drawing closer drowned out even the high-pitched scream of the security perimeter alarm.

The radio on Gavin's hip crackled. He answered, "What have you found?"

Brian's voice came across the line. "Three hundred yards due north we found a break in the fence line."

"We're heading your way," Gavin said as he and Lucas both turned, going back the way they'd come.

There was that noise again, just barely discernible over the sirens. The unease and trepidation mounting through Lucas became a tsunami demanding he assess what he'd heard moments before the sirens. He stopped, closed his eyes and used every sense he could, listening and filtering through the sirens and the alarm to find the noise again.

A helicopter.

His gaze searched the darkened sky. Stars winked out, then reappeared as something dark streaked across the night sky.

"Inbound helicopter," Lucas shouted, running toward the house. "The fence was a diversion."

To lure the marshals away from the house so Colin could kill Paige. Grateful to his boss for the extreme security measure of the safe bunker under the barn, Lucas said, "The house. They're going to blow it."

Colin had already proved his had a grenade launcher back at the Beales' house.

"We have to bring down the chopper," Gavin shouted.

Wind and debris whipped up by the rotors of the helicopter as it descended slightly bit at Lucas. He had to disable the helicopter and keep the occupants from doing anything that would hurt the people he loved.

FIFTEEN

Lucas dropped to one knee, aimed the rifle at the helicopter and fired. He couldn't be sure if he hit the metal bird through the chaos of noise from the rotors and the emergency vehicles arriving.

A barrage of gunfire slammed into the dirt around him, barely missing him. He dove to the side and scrambled behind the SUVs.

The familiar high-pitched whine of an RPG filled the air. A rocket-launched grenade streaked through the air. A bright light of destruction headed for the main house.

Stomach plummeting, Lucas sighted the helicopter again, but the helo repositioned just as he fired. And the house exploded. The cacophony of noise battered at his eardrums. A large gaping hole appeared on the side of the house facing the helicopter. Orange and yellow flames shot into the air. Blasts of heat buffeted him as he ducked down. Debris from the explosion scattered across the front yard.

Heart hammering, he thanked God above that Paige, Kenny, Aslan, Victoria and Adele were safe underground.

Around him, police officers, as well as Gavin and Brian, fired at the helicopter. It lifted high, zooming away and then zooming back to launch another grenade.

This time, the horse barn was the target. The wooden

structure shattered and burst into fiery flames, adding to the heat and noise.

Panic slammed into Lucas. Would those inside the bunker survive?

Several loud explosions echoed through the underground bunker. Paige tightened her hold on Kenny. The corner of the papers inside the satchel still hanging across her body poked at her. She winced. The file that had incited this mess. She wanted to rip it to shreds. But that wouldn't reverse time. It wouldn't return her life to normal. Nor would it have stopped Donald's death.

The muted sounds of sirens and gunfire raised the hairs on the back of her neck and terror slid along her limbs.

"This is all my fault," Paige said, her voice catching. She buried her face in her son's soft hair.

Victoria moved to sit beside Paige and wrapped her arms around her and Kenny. "This is not your fault. This is no one's fault. Bad people do bad things."

"You don't understand," Paige sobbed. "I called my father. I don't know how, but the bad people must have traced the call and found us."

"Nonsense. I'm sure you're not the only one who made phone calls from here," Victoria said.

Adele stopped pacing, her eyes growing round. "I made a call, too. I called my personal assistant as soon as we arrived. Obviously, it's public knowledge that I'm married to a deputy US marshal. And if the assassin after you was watching the whole team, they could have traced my call, or pinged my phone, or they could have simply followed Brian and me here."

Paige didn't believe for a minute Brian wouldn't have spotted a tail. The deputies were good at their jobs. And though she appreciated both women trying to massage her guilt, she knew this came down to her betraying Lucas's trust and not listening to his sound advice. She'd been selfish.

The air in the bunker grew heavy. Paige released Kenny and tugged at the collar of her shirt. "It's hot down here."

Victoria rose and crossed the bunker to grab bottles of water. She passed them out. "Keep hydrated. It might be a while." Then she was thoughtful enough to fill a bowl with water and set it down for Aslan, still pressed tight against her and Kenny's legs. The dog lapped up the liquid, sloshing some over the sides.

Paige's stomach turned and the water did nothing to alleviate the nausea rolling through her system. Lucas was out there, possibly injured, maybe even dead. Putting him and the others in mortal danger would hang over her head for the rest of her life. She silently lifted a prayer to God. *Please, don't let this be the end.*

Lucas raced to where he'd seen a hose hooked up to a spout on the side of the house that was still intact, praying the hose would be long enough to reach the barn. Smoke curled around him, burning his eyes and throat, making him cough. Heat prickled his skin and threatened to melt his shirt to his back. But the only thing Lucas could concentrate on was putting out the barn fire and rescuing Paige, Kenny and the others.

Gavin hurried over to help. "You crank the water and I'll hold the hose."

"The fire department is on its way," Brian said as he rushed up to help Gavin unwind the length of the hose.

Duncan and Sera ran over, also.

"We'll track the helicopter," Sera said. Without waiting for affirmation, the pair turned and sped to one of the SUVs. They had to knock off burning debris before firing up the engine and leaving the ranch in a spray of gravel.

Lucas didn't know how they intended to find and follow the helicopter, but that wasn't his concern at the moment. He needed to put the fire out over the barn so he could release Paige, Kenny, Aslan, Victoria and Adele.

Gavin barked out orders to the other police officers offering a hand. "Grab buckets. There's water in the troughs."

Lucas felt helpless as they combated the fire consuming the barn. With so much hay and wood, the flames refused to relinquish their hold on the structure.

The arrival of the fire department brought hope. Lucas tried to help but was commanded back as the firefighters used specialized foam to blanket the barn, smothering the flames and extinguishing the fire.

Without waiting for the fire department to give permission to enter the burned barn, Lucas and Brian raced to the charred remains. Working together, they had to push aside fallen beams to uncover the trapdoor. They lifted the hatched.

"Adele," Brian yelled. "I'm coming down." Brian disappeared into the underground bunker.

Lucas held his breath, his body vibrating with tension as he waited for the ladies and child to come out. Aslan's barks punctuated the air.

Victoria climbed out, then Adele followed by Paige and Kenny. Their faces were drained of color and their eyes wide with fear, but otherwise they seemed unharmed.

While Kenny remained at the bunker opening, talking encouragingly down to Aslan, Paige walked straight to Lucas and wrapped her arms around him, hugging him tightly. "I was so scared something had happened to you."

Heart beating in his throat, he hugged her back before releasing her. "I was concerned for you."

Kenny ran to them, flinging his arms around Lucas's waist and squeezing tight. Lucas smoothed a hand over the boy's thin shoulders, grateful that both mother and child were unharmed.

"Need a little help here," Brian called from inside the bunker.

Lucas disengaged from Kenny. Gavin appeared and ushered the ladies out of the charred debris of the barn while Lucas moved to help Brian with Aslan. Brian lifted the dog up and Lucas reached into the opening to grab ahold of Aslan and brought him out of the bunker. Brian climbed up behind the dog.

Aslan licked Lucas's face.

"I'm glad to see you, too, boy," Lucas murmured, and carried the dog away from the area to where the others had gathered. He set Aslan on the ground. Then Lucas took hold of Paige's elbow and Kenny's hand. "You two need to get a safe distance away from the fire. Come with me."

"Wow, the house is on fire!" Kenny exclaimed. "That's not good."

"What happened? It's like a war zone." Paige's voice shook, and a tremor raced through her beneath his hand on her elbow.

"More RPGs," he told her, not wanting to sugarcoat the situation. "From a helicopter."

Paige leaned into him. "I guess that's what happens when an arms dealer wants you dead. I'm so sorry for the loss of the Armstrongs' ranch."

"Me, too," he said and flagged down a young San Antonio police officer and redirected his attention from helping to contain the fire. "Officer, I need you to do something for me. Your job right now—your only, most important job—is to watch over these three," Lucas said, indicating Paige, Kenny and Aslan.

Solemnly, the police officer nodded. "Yes, sir."

Paige grabbed the sleeve of his plaid shirt. "Lucas, don't leave us."

"You'll be safe here with the officer," he assured her. "I have to help Gavin save the cabins."

Confident that the three would be safe with the patrolman, Lucas hustled back to help douse the fire.

Paige watched the chaos in front of her with a mixture of horror and despair. Everyone from the firemen to the US marshals were working to quell the blaze. Even Adele and Victoria used buckets to pull water from the horse troughs near the pasture. Feeling useless and guilty, Paige itched to help.

"Mama, are the horses okay?" Kenny asked, drawing her attention.

"I'm sure they're fine, honey. They let them out into the back pasture. They'll stay away from the fire," she said, hoping it was true.

"I can go check on them," Kenny offered.

"Sweetie, listen—"

Shouts diverted her attention away from Kenny to where flames licked the wall of the closest cabin to the house.

Paige couldn't stand it anymore. She had to help. To the patrol officer, she said, "We can't just stand here. They need more bodies."

The patrolman shook his head. "The deputy told me to stay close to you and keep you back. That's what I am doing."

Frustration ran through Paige, but she knew she couldn't defy Lucas's instructions again. The last time she had defied him, it had resulted in this catastrophe.

She turned to talk to Kenny, only he wasn't there. Neither was Aslan.

"Kenny!" Heart pounding in her throat, she searched around the vehicle, but Kenny and Aslan were nowhere to be found. She replayed his earlier comment. Her heart dropped to her toes. He'd gone to the pasture to check on the horses. She grabbed the patrolman by the arm and dragged him with her. "We have to find my son."

Out of his peripheral vision, Lucas saw Paige and the patrolman running away from the area toward the back pasture. He ground his teeth with frustration. What were they doing? Where was Kenny and Aslan? Dread, sickening and thick, settled in his gut.

Lucas took off at a run in the direction where he'd seen Paige headed. He caught up to them. "Hey! Paige!"

"Kenny!" she shouted, ignoring Lucas.

Anguish gripped him by the throat. "Where's Kenny?"

"He disappeared," the patrolman offered, sweeping a flashlight over the area. "He was there one second and gone the next."

"He wanted to check on the horses," Paige said, her voice filled with fear. "Kenny!"

Aslan charged toward them. The dog crashed into Lucas. In his mouth, he held a scrap of bloody fabric.

Lucas took the material from Aslan.

Black tactical.

A shudder of horror ripped through Lucas. He grabbed Paige by the biceps. "Go back with the patrolman. Tell the others. I will go after Kenny."

"No! He needs me." Panic threaded through her voice.

"Paige, I can't worry about you and Kenny," he told her.

"Then don't worry about me," she said, stalking off in the direction of the back pasture.

Lucas growled in frustration. "Wait!"

She paused, wrapping her arms around her middle.

To the patrolman, he said, "Let me have your flashlight.

Call this in. We need backup." Then to Aslan, Lucas urged, "Find Kenny."

The dog took off, back in the direction he'd come from, disappearing into the dark pasture. Lucas and Paige ran after him. Lucas wished he had night vision goggles, but the borrowed flashlight would have to do. He swept the light in a wide arc, looking for signs of the boy. The horses whinnied as they ran past them.

"Kenny!" Paige yelled again.

Aslan led them to a break in the electric fence lining the property. A break they hadn't found before the helicopter showed up.

On the other side of the fence, there were tire marks.

Fresh horror blossomed through Lucas's chest. Agony, hot and sharp, threatened to slash him apart.

Kenny had been abducted.

The patrol officer ran up. "Others are on their way."

Paige fell to her knees with a sob. "They took Kenny."

Aslan whimpered as he stared at the broken fence.

Lucas knelt beside Paige and gathered her close. Cupping her face, he met her gaze in the glow from the officer's flashlight. "I promise you I will move Heaven and earth to find Kenny and bring him home to you."

She nodded, then shook her head as more sobs escaped. "You don't understand. My fault." She collapsed against him.

"Paige, honey, this is not on you," Lucas told her. "If anyone's to blame, it's me. I should've stayed with you like you'd asked me to."

"I called my father," she said, her voice muffled against his shoulder.

A rush of understanding had him tightening his arms around her. Of course, she'd used the burner phone he'd bought for her. He should have remembered the device earlier. If he'd been better prepared, this wouldn't have happened. Guilt bunched up his muscles.

Playing the blame game wouldn't help either of them. They needed to focus on pulling themselves together and finding Kenny. "There's no way anyone could trace those phones. They'd have to be in law enforcement, obtain a warrant to search cell activity, plus have a specialized system to be able to pinpoint our location so exactly."

Paige lifted her head. "Bad people do bad things."

He grimaced. "You're right, of course." Who knew about the burner phones? He tucked the question away as Sera and Duncan rushed to their side.

"We heard about Kenny," Sera said.

"We followed the helicopter but lost it over the hills. That bird wasn't a civilian issue," Duncan said.

"It was military," Sera said. "But I'd say mercenaries, rather than armed forces."

Then something occurred to him. "The lawyer," Lucas said. "She's the unknown here. It has to be her operation."

"It's possible she'd have the connections to orchestrate an operation like this," Duncan said.

Gavin, Victoria, Brian and Adele rushed up, each carrying flashlights.

"I put out a missing child report," Gavin said. "Law enforcement across the state will be searching for Kenny."

"I need to get Paige to a safe location while we search for Kenny," Lucas said.

Paige made a noise of dissent.

"The lake house," Brian and Adele said.

"Simon's apartment," Duncan and Sera said.

Lucas stared at the two couples. Each in unison had referred to a location that had served as a safe place in the past.

"We'll have the police escort us back to the station," Gavin said. "Then we'll make plans to relocate."

Lucas helped Paige to her feet.

"There are tire tracks," Lucas said, gesturing to the other side of the electric fence.

"We'll see if we can follow the tracks," Sera said, already moving to the fence. In long strides, Duncan was at her side.

Lucas appreciated having a team. There was no way he could find Kenny on his own. He sent up a prayer of gratitude and a plea. *Lord, don't let anything happen to Kenny.*

In the dark interior of the SUV, Paige clutched her satchel to her chest with Aslan at her feet, his nose on her knees. The rush of adrenaline and fear made her body weak. She wasn't sure how she was staying upright. She wanted to melt into a puddle but that would do no one any good. Least of all her son.

Gavin drove and Victoria sat in the passenger seat.

Sitting in the back beside Paige, Lucas made a call. The low murmur of his voice soothed the edges of her fear. She clung to his promise to find Kenny.

Tears filled her eyes and torment clutched at her throat, making swallowing difficult. She prayed he wasn't being hurt.

Oh, no. What if he had a seizure?

She squeezed her eyes shut and pleaded with God.

The phone inside the satchel vibrated. She was thankful she'd put the ringer on silent. Her father calling her back?

She itched to answer but decided it would be best not to, even though she longed to hear her father's voice. It would only distress him to know that Kenny was missing.

Every few minutes, the phone vibrated. Too afraid to move, too afraid to peek inside and look at the phone, she continued to ignore the calls.

When they reached the Marshals' headquarters, she excused herself and hurried toward the restroom. Lucas followed her.

Pausing outside the door, she said, "You don't need to babysit me."

Lucas raised his hands. "I just want you to feel safe."

She couldn't fault him. "I'll only be a minute."

He gave a nod, his cowboy hat tinged black from the fire. The sight made her stomach clench.

Inside the three-stall restroom, she went to the sink and placed the satchel on the counter. The phone vibrating ratcheted up the tension in her body. After checking that there was no one else in the room, she fished the phone out of the bag. She stared at the unknown number. Not her father.

She saw there was a text message.

The words screamed out at her from the small little screen.

If you want to see your son alive, ditch your security and come to this address. Bring the file.

She swallowed back her apprehension. Clearly, the bad people knew her phone number. Had something happened to her dad, too?

Her knees buckled.

Clutching the counter to stay upright, she struggled to think.

She had no way to get to where the kidnappers wanted her to go. But her son's life was on the line. She had to find a way to get there. But then what? They kill her and Kenny?

There was only one course of action.

She had to fully trust Lucas.

SIXTEEN

Lucas waited for Paige outside the restroom and stared at the smudges on his hat. A shiver ran over him. The events of the night were like a bad B movie. Only the film was still running. Kenny had been kidnapped.

How had this happened?

"Hey," Sera called to him as she and her husband, Duncan, came out of the elevator and moved with purpose toward him.

A flare of hope burned in Lucas. "Kenny?"

Sera shook her head, frustration evident in the tight line of her mouth and the hard glint in her dark eyes.

"We followed the tire tracks to the highway," Duncan said, referring to the marks they'd found on the opposite side of the electric fence line where Kenny had been kidnapped.

What little hope he'd had fizzled. This would further devastate Paige. Lucas glanced toward the restroom door.

"Without knowing what kind of vehicle they were using," Sera said, "we have no way of knowing which direction they went or where they are holing up."

Aggravation pounded behind Lucas's eyes as he returned his focus to his colleagues. "We have to find Kenny. The idea of Colin with the boy makes my blood run cold."

"Boss put out an alert with every law enforcement agency

in the state." Sera put a hand on his forearm. "We can't lose hope."

Good advice, only Lucas was struggling to keep despair at bay.

The door to the restroom opened and Paige walked out. The wrecked expression on her face had his stomach churning. She was terrified. Who could blame her? Aslan stayed close to her side, clearly sensing her distress. Or maybe the dog was trying to ease his own distress.

Paige focused on Sera and Duncan. Anticipation flared in her eyes. "Any news on Kenny?"

"No, I'm sorry," Sera said. "But I was just saying to Lucas we can't give up hope."

Shoulders slumping slightly, Paige nodded. "Thank you." She turned her glassy-eyed gaze to Lucas. "Is there somewhere I can get a cup of coffee?"

"We can take you to the hotel where Victoria and Adele are staying," Sera said. "It's just down the road and very secure. Brian arranged for SAPD to have men posted inside and out."

"I can't leave until we find Kenny," Paige answered. She turned her attention back to Lucas. "Coffee."

There was an intensity to her expression and the way she emphasized the word that had him on edge. She wanted something more than coffee. "Of course," Lucas said. "The break room. This way."

He put his hand to the small of her back, feeling her tremble beneath his fingers. Aslan's nails clicked on the tile floor as they entered the break room, which was thankfully empty.

Aslan sniffed around the room, then moved to sit by the door as if waiting for Kenny.

Lucas headed for the coffee machine, but Paige snagged his arm, stopping him in his tracks.

"I need to tell you something," she said, her voice lowered as she glanced toward the door. "But it's for your ears only."

Taken aback, Lucas covered her hand with his own. "You can tell me anything. We're safe here."

She took a shuddering breath and then blurted. "They texted me."

He couldn't have heard her correctly. "What?"

"The people who have my son," she said. "They want me to come to some address by myself. With the file. They said I have to be alone." Her voice broke but she swallowed before continuing. "If they see anyone else, they'll kill him. They'll kill my baby."

Her words were like a knife to his chest. "Let me see the text."

Aslan walked over and lay down at Paige's feet.

Setting her satchel on the table, she dug out the phone and handed it to him. The message was just as she'd said. "How does he know about the file?"

She grimaced. "When Colin had a gun to my head, I told him about the file thinking it would keep him from killing me."

His stomach curdled. "Do you trust me?"

"Of course. That's why I'm telling you. We need a car." The urgency in her voice tore at him.

"I need to tell the team. We'll need backup," he told her.

"No." She stepped away from him. Aslan scrambled to his feet. "They said to come alone. I can't risk Kenny's life."

He took her hand. "If we go there without support, we may end up dead," he told her. "The only way this works is with the team. The only way we get Kenny back is with the team."

She yanked her hand from his and pulled the manila

envelope from her satchel. "Why haven't you told anyone here about this file?"

Guilt pricked him. "My former task force leader ordered me to keep it confidential. But I have to tell Gavin about the file and the text. I trust him and the team with my life. They are as close as family."

Her gaze narrowed. "We've been hunted and tracked from the beginning. Long before I called my father."

The truth in her words raised his blood pressure. "James believes there's a mole somewhere in the pipeline. He's working on discovering who."

She cocked her head. "James. The man you called after we were ambushed at the airport?"

"Yes. My former task force leader."

She waved the envelope at him. "Who knew we were going to be there at the airport?"

Something akin to dread crimped his chest. "The FBI, Gavin and James."

"Who knew our route out of Florida?"

That dread turned to suspicion and anger. "Gavin and James. And the FBI."

"The FBI was waiting for us here. Could they have planted that smoke bomb? I had the distinct feeling they were trying to take me away when Colin showed up."

Lucas could see where she was going with her questions. Yet, his mind rebelled. "I refuse to believe someone close to the investigation is feeding intel to Colin."

But he'd never worked with the FBI agents before now. Could Agent McIntosh be the leak? Could he be working with Colin?

What about McIntosh's boss, Special Agent in Charge Von Amici?

She frowned and shook her head. "But Colin did show

up. The FBI agents protected me from him. So who tipped The Beast off?"

The question reverberated through Lucas's brain. Who, indeed? A wave of nausea swept through him. As much as he hated to accept it, it had to be someone close.

Again, she waved the envelope. "What is in this that someone doesn't want brought to light?"

"Good question." Lucas's fingers closed over the envelope. "The best way for us to rescue Kenny is to figure out who has him and why."

Lucas sat and read each sheet of paper before handing them over to Paige. The case was pretty straightforward with the evidence and intel the task force had gathered. He saw Paige's initials at the bottom of each paper. "You typed this up?"

"I did. At least the pages that have my initials."

Lucas continued reading through the supporting evidence regarding the charges brought against Adam Wayne. At the bottom of one sheet of paper, there was a handwritten note. The cursive was hard to make out. Lucas turned it for Paige to see. "Is this your writing?"

"No, that's Donald's." She studied the words. "He had atrocious handwriting. I believe this says *connection between Adam Wayne and J. Barlow. Need further investigation.*"

Lucas's breath stalled in his chest. "That can't be right. What evidence?" He looked through the rest of the file, but there was no other mention of James Barlow. "I don't understand. Why would Donald write that? Who was this supposed to go to?"

Had Lucas trusted the wrong person? Yet, James being in league with the arms dealer made sense in a twisted way. The task force had had such a hard time catching a break until finally all the dominoes neatly lined up and they had enough incriminating evidence against Wayne.

Too neatly, in retrospect.

Had James sacrificed Wayne? What was going on here? It was past time to come clean with Gavin. Lucas would accept the consequences, but he couldn't let Kenny and Paige pay for his misplaced trust.

"Lucas, what does all this mean?"

"It means I messed up royally." He gathered the case file, slipping it back into the envelope. He'd been blind. He shoved the papers back into the satchel. "We need to talk to Gavin."

Handing her the satchel, he led her out of the break room and down the hall to his boss's office. Aslan stuck close to Paige's side.

Gavin wasn't alone.

James Barlow was standing in the office.

Lucas stopped short, Paige bumping into him. Lucas tucked Paige into his side and pushed the satchel out of view. Aslan squeezed past them and sniffed at James. Lucas held his breath. Would the dog smell Kenny?

When the dog dismissed James and returned to Paige's side, Lucas said, "James! You're here."

"I told you I was on my way," James said, giving Aslan a curious glance. Dressed as always in a custom-tailored suit of charcoal gray, he was a tall imposing man with a lean build, dark intense eyes and a chiseled jaw. "I was just filling the marshal in on why I'm here."

Lucas mentally winced but met Gavin's gaze and willed him to understand. "I have a lot to explain."

"Indeed, you do," Gavin said, his voice hard. "What is this file James was telling me about?"

"We discovered that Paige had a hard copy of the Adam

Wayne case file," Lucas said. "Unfortunately, it was destroyed in the ranch fire."

From his periphery, Lucas noted Paige's startled gaze, but he kept his focus locked on Gavin and prayed she didn't say anything to alert James of the deception. The file and the knowledge that James was somehow connected to Wayne was the only leverage they had. If James thought he was in the clear, then maybe he'd order Kenny released. One could hope.

Gavin arched an eyebrow but didn't comment.

"That's too bad," James said, his penetrating gaze drawing Lucas's attention. "This was a wasted trip. You should have told me."

"We've been in crisis mode," Lucas said, unable to keep his voice from dripping with anger. "Kenny Walsh was abducted from the ranch."

James's expression didn't alter. "I hadn't heard." He shifted his attention to Paige. "Have the kidnappers contacted you?"

Lucas gave her a squeeze with his arm. "No."

She shook her head, affirming his statement.

"That's unfortunate." Something flickered in James's eyes. "The Transnational Organized Crime Mission Center is at your disposal."

Lucas said, "We could use the help to locate Colin. We believe he and Eliza Mendez, the mastermind behind the operation, are working together." He hoped by keeping up the pretense they thought Eliza was the one in charge, James wouldn't be suspicious and do anything drastic.

"I'll pull resources," James said. "We'll find them."

"The address I gave you earlier," Lucas said, curious how the man would react. "Who did it belong to?"

James shook his head and shrugged. "It was a bogus address."

"That's too bad," Lucas said, repeating what James had said earlier.

There was an intensity in James's gaze and Lucas set up a prayer that he had not given away his knowledge that somehow James was in league with Adam Wayne.

After a beat, James turned to Gavin. "I'll be in touch."

James strode past Lucas and Paige, exiting the office. Lucas watched until the man entered the elevator and the door shut behind him. Lucas leaned against the doorjamb as the ramifications of what he was about to say slammed into him.

"Explain," Gavin said, his voice razor-sharp.

Pushing away from the door, Lucas straightened his shoulders. "Not here. The armory."

Not giving his boss a chance to protest, Lucas pivoted with Paige still locked against him and exited the office. As they walked through the main office, Lucas said, "Sera, we need you. Bring your laptop. Get Brian."

Duncan rose. "I guess that's my cue to bug out."

Over his shoulder, Lucas said, "No. You, too. We need everyone."

Paige wasn't quite sure what was happening but remained silent as she allowed Lucas to escort her and Aslan down a flight of stairs and into a locked room with no windows. The armory was just as the name sounded. There were rows and rows of firearms and tactical gear. Lockers against one wall and benches for the deputies to sit on. Lucas released her and she sat on one of the benches, gripping the satchel to her side.

They waited as Gavin, followed by Sera and Duncan, entered.

"Brian and Jace will be here in a minute," Sera said.

"Where's Joe?" Lucas asked.

"He's with Brian and Jace," Sera said. "Joe picked up Jace and Abby from the airport and took them directly to the hotel."

"Who's Joe?" Paige asked, not liking the idea of there being more people she had to trust her son's life to.

"He's a rookie deputy," Lucas replied. "Joe's on the up and up."

She barely contained a snort. Being assured of the character of a person she'd never met wasn't high on her list of believable scenarios at the moment. But she did trust Lucas.

Gavin leaned against the lockers. "This better be good. Tell me, is my wife in jeopardy?"

"Not as far as we know," Lucas said. "She and Adele are safe."

Paige took the opportunity to apologize to Gavin. "I'm sorry, sir, to have brought all this on you and your team. Because of me, you lost your home."

Gavin's expression softened. "Victoria told me you felt responsible. We lay blame where it really belongs. On those who committed the crimes."

His generosity was a balm to her guilt, but nothing could make the fear and worry running rampant through her dissipate. Only having Kenny by her side would allow her to feel any peace. As if sensing her upset, Aslan laid his head on her lap. She buried her fingers in his soft fur. Tears burned the backs of her eyes, but she blinked to keep them from falling. She wanted her son.

A moment later, the door to the armory opened and three more deputies filed in. Paige smiled a greeting at Brian but the other two men were strangers.

The younger of the two halted. His dark hair curled around his ears and a curious expression bloomed on his face. "Should I be here?"

"Yes," Lucas said. "Shut the door."

The tall blond man who resembled Gavin had to be his son. He raised an eyebrow. "I'm sorry we haven't met. I'm Jace Armstrong." He stepped forward and extended his hand.

Paige took it and nodded. "I wish I were meeting you under better circumstances."

"Me, too." Jace released her and turned to his father. "Abby is with Mom and Adele at the hotel. Care to explain what's happening?"

"This is Lucas's show," Gavin said.

Paige could see the tension in Lucas's shoulders. She didn't know how to make this better for him. Or if she even could.

"From the beginning, we have been working under the assumption that Colin was hunting Paige because she witnessed him kill Donald Lessing," Lucas began. "But she also had in her possession a hard copy of the case file against Adam Wayne that Donald Lessing was going to present in court."

"So, Adam Wayne has been behind the attacks?" Brian asked.

"I thought we decided it was Eliza Mendez who was the mastermind," Sera said.

"We are wrong on both accounts. The case file indicates that Donald Lessing believed there was a connection between Wayne and Homeland Security Agent James Barlow."

Paige sucked in a breath. J. Barlow was James, the man she had just met in Gavin's office. No wonder Lucas had been so upset.

Gavin pushed away from the lockers and widened his stance, folding his arms over his chest. "Are we really to believe the new head of Homeland Security's Transnational Organized Crime Mission Center is the one pulling Colin's strings?"

"Paige, the file." Lucas held out his hand.

Paige retrieved the manila envelope containing the case file out of the satchel and handed it over. Lucas held it out to his boss. "Donald Lessing had made a connection. I believe that is what got him killed."

Sera reached for the envelope. "There's an address here with no name."

Paige said, "That was why I had gone to Donald's office the night he was killed. I don't know who he intended to receive this file."

Sera's fingers flew over her laptop keyboard. Then she handed the envelope to Brian, who slipped the contents out of the envelope and thumbed through them.

"Are we meeting here because you believe James bugged my office?" Gavin asked.

Lucas nodded. "I didn't want to take the chance. Unfortunately, I've been keeping him informed of our every move. He knew we were here at headquarters. He asked Paige outright if the kidnappers had contacted her. He knew very well that they had."

"Excuse me?" Gavin's scowl was intimidating as his gaze bounced from Lucas to Paige and back again.

Paige extracted the burner phone from her satchel and held it out. "I received a text telling me to meet at an address if I wanted to see my son alive again."

Jace took the phone from her, reading the text. He showed the text to the others.

Gavin shook his head. "I get that your loyalties, Deputy Cavendish, were divided. What assurance do I have that from this point forward you stay committed to this team?"

"You have my word, sir," Lucas said. "I was duped. It won't happen again."

"It better not or you will be looking for a new job," Gavin stated in a voice filled with anger.

Paige hated that she'd caused this to happen. But she needed these people to find her son.

"That address on the envelope belongs to the private residence in DC of the secretary of Homeland Security," Sera said. "James's boss."

"Donald Lessing was going to blow the whistle on James," Lucas stated.

"I should have just mailed that envelope." Recriminations pounded at Paige. Then she and Kenny would be safe at home.

But she'd never have met Lucas.

And James and Colin and Eliza would have killed Donald, and no one would have been the wiser.

Lucas moved to sit beside her and took her hand. "We can't undo the past. We can only move forward in faith." To Gavin, Lucas said, "Sir, Kenny is the priority here. We have to find him."

Paige's heart melted and she clung to Lucas's hand as love for this man flooded every fiber of her being. She clamped her lips together to keep from blurting out her feelings. Now was not the time or place. And she had no guarantee there would ever be a right time and place.

Sera held out her hand for the phone. "Let me check the address they want her to go to."

The room was silent except for the clicking of Sera's fingers on the keyboard of her laptop. "Got it. It's an old farm on the outskirts of town. It's in foreclosure so it should be abandoned. The perfect spot for an ambush."

"Then that's what we will do," Gavin said.

Paige stood, her hand still encased in Lucas's. "Sir, use me as bait."

Lucas jumped to his feet. "No. I'm not putting you in harm's way."

Paige squeezed his hand. "I have to do this. You'll have my back."

"*We* will have your back," Brian said.

There was a murmur of agreement among the other deputies.

Gavin met her gaze. "As much as I appreciate the offer, no."

"I will do anything for my son," Paige told him, infusing passion into her voice.

"The best thing you can do for your son is let us do our job," Gavin stated. "Everyone, gear up." To Lucas, he said, "You and Brian take her to the hotel, then meet us. I'm calling in SAPD's SWAT team."

As the deputies around her began grabbing weapons and tactical equipment, Lucas recaptured both her hands and met her gaze. "You are a brave woman."

He pulled her close and kissed her right there in front of everyone. For the briefest second, her fear eased. She felt cared for and protected. If anyone could bring back her child, it was this man.

By kissing her in front of his work family, was he making a declaration? Whether he was or not, she couldn't worry about it now.

She'd tackle the question of their future later.

The sound of a throat clearing forced them apart.

Sera grinned and thrust a flak vest at Lucas. "Put this on, lover boy."

The heat of embarrassment flushed through Paige's cheeks. But she fisted her hands in Lucas's shirt. "Bring my son back to me."

"I promise." Carrying the flak vest, Lucas urged her and Aslan to the door. "Let's go."

SEVENTEEN

Nervous jitters plagued Paige all the way from the Marshals offices to the large national brand hotel a block away. Brian and Lucas escorted her into the building and up the elevator to the top floor. Brian stayed at the elevator while Lucas walked her down the hall to the presidential suite where two armed police officers stood guard outside the door.

Pausing mid-stride, she broke the awkward silence that had fallen between them. She fished Kenny's medication out of her satchel and handed it to Lucas. "Just in case," her voice hitched.

Taking the medication and stowing it in his pocket, he said, "You're a good mother."

Guilt for kissing Lucas and for not giving every moment and every fiber of her being to thoughts of Kenny had her insides tied up. But she knew this worry and anxiety was only harming her. It would do nothing to bring Kenny back. The only possibility she had of being reunited with her son was her faith in God and her confidence in Lucas and the team of men and women dedicated to justice and serving the people. People like her and Kenny. "Please, be careful."

Lucas touched her cheek. "I will be careful. And I will bring Kenny back. Then we can talk about the future."

She wanted to hold on to his words as a promise for a

future together. But doubts crowded in. What-if scenarios brimming with doom and gloom surfaced, knocking at her mind and wanting to fill her with despair. With determination, she resisted the temptation to give in to the horrors at the edges of her consciousness waiting to pounce.

She wouldn't lose hope.

She would lean on her faith.

She would trust Lucas.

Gripping his hand, she brought his knuckles to her lips. "Just return to me. Bring my son with you."

He squeezed her hand and then moved her to the door where he knocked loudly.

The door immediately opened. Victoria stepped out, spreading her arms wide for Paige. Overcome with emotion, Paige practically collapsed into the woman's embrace. Victoria's soothing hand on her back reminded Paige of her own mother.

"We'll take care of her, Caveman," Victoria said. "You all come back to us safely. Godspeed."

"Yes, ma'am," Lucas said.

Then Victoria pulled Paige into the hotel suite, shutting the door behind them. Paige tried not to shudder at the finality of the lock sliding into place.

Lucas and Brian made good time to the meetup place a mile from the property location texted to Paige. Anticipation combined with the late afternoon sunlight beating down on them caused sweat to bead beneath Lucas's flak vest. True to his word, Gavin had gathered the SAPD SWAT team, six men and women dressed in black tactical body armor and carrying heavy firepower. Several FBI agents, including McIntosh and Von Amici, were present wearing their dark blue windbreakers with the big yellow letters emblazoned on the back and covering their own flak vests.

McIntosh hustled forward to meet Lucas. "Your boss filled us in. Unbelievable. Who would've thought James Barlow would betray his country."

Lucas refrained from telling the man he'd suspected him at one point. That would do no good. He needed the goodwill of the FBI to make sure that when they captured James, Colin and the others they never saw the light of day again.

"Now we have a chance to bring him to justice," Lucas replied. With a good-luck pat on McIntosh's shoulder, he peeled away to hustle over to where Gavin and the SWAT command leader, a tall man with broad shoulders beneath his body armor, stood staring at a screen. Gavin made room for Lucas.

"We have a drone circling the property," Gavin told him. "It looks like the house is nothing more than a few beams and studs. But this large rickety-looking barn shows heat signatures."

Blood spiking at the information, Lucas asked, "Kenny?"

"It appears the child is in the northeast corner," the SWAT command leader said. "Here." He pointed to the screen.

Lucas's gut clenched at the sight of the reddish glowing outline of a small child. He seemed to be sitting on something above the ground with his knees drawn to his chest. Lucas sent up a silent prayer that the boy wasn't having a seizure. That he was staying strong. And that Lucas would get to him in time. He patted his pocket, reassuring himself he had the means to help Kenny if needed.

"What's the plan?" Brian said as he joined them.

"Sera will pretend to be Paige," Gavin said. "She will arrive in an SUV and park near the barn doors. Duncan and Jace will be hiding in the rear, ready to pounce."

"SWAT and FBI will circle the perimeter and move inward, ready to seize the building once the boy is secure."

Lucas met his boss's gaze. "I'm going in for Kenny."

One side of Gavin's mouth tipped up in a wry smile. "I would've been surprised had you not volunteered."

"The boy knows me," Lucas said, hoping to waylay any protests. "Anyone else might scare him. I'm the only chance we have of getting him out of there quietly. Safely."

Gavin held up his hands. "Hold your horses, Caveman. You're going in."

Lucas breathed a sigh of relief that he didn't have to continue to argue the point.

Brian clapped Lucas on the shoulder. "I'll go with you. I told your lady we'd have your back."

Something inside of Lucas shifted. His lady. Paige was his. He'd been wrong to hold himself apart. It was wrong to deny himself a relationship with a woman as amazing as Paige and a kid as adorable as Kenny. He had to have faith enough to trust that God would keep them all safe.

If Paige would have him, he couldn't wait to spend the rest of his life showing her how precious and loved she was. But for now, he had to push all thoughts of her aside so he could concentrate on what he needed to do without distractions. Kenny was the priority here.

"Are there guards at the back doors?" he asked.

"Affirmative," the SWAT command leader said. "There's a hayloft glassless window here on the northeast corner above where the boy is sitting. You can scale the wall and drop inside without being seen. You get the boy secured, then we breach."

Lucas didn't waste time approving the plan as he allowed a SWAT team member to rig him up with a harness, a plastic grappling hook that wouldn't make noise when it clamped on and black nylon rope for scaling the barn wall.

Lucas caught a glimpse of Sera wearing a blond wig. The color was wrong. Paige was more strawberry than platinum. Lucas sent up a prayer that the difference wouldn't be noticed from outside the SUV. Sera gave him a thumbs-up. He returned the gesture. Gratitude for these people filled him with confidence. They would be successful. They had to be. Failure wasn't an option.

He and Brian hustled down the road, letting the tall weeds cloak them as they made their way around the broken and disintegrating wooden property fence line.

In his ear, Lucas heard the SWAT command leader say, "Your approach is clear."

Lucas and Brian hustled through the broken slats of the fence into the gone-to-seed pasture, running in a low crouch.

As they approached the dilapidated house, Lucas asked, "Anyone hiding inside the main structure?"

"No heat signatures," came back the reply.

Confident the drone would pick up any stray bogeys hiding out in the remains of the ranch house, Lucas and Brian hurried across what would have been the backyard and was now a patchy mess of dirt and grass. They hid behind a propane tank where they had a clear view of the northeast side of the barn and the hayloft window.

Brian held out his fist. Lucas bumped it with his own.

"I'll watch your six from out here," Brian told him. "Once you're inside, be careful."

"In and out before they even realize it," Lucas said with assurance, praying the confidence he felt inside his heart would hold true.

In a low crouch, Lucas ran to the northeast side of the barn. He didn't hesitate. Time was of the essence. He took the grappling hook tied to the rope and twirled it in the air, then flung it up to the top of the window. The hook soundlessly grabbed onto the windowsill. He tested the rope. Satisfied it would hold him, he scaled up the barn wall.

When he reached the open window frame, he gripped the edges and peeked over. Then said in a low voice, "I have a visual on James Barlow and Colin Richter."

"The feds discovered a helicopter waiting for James and Colin a mile away," Gavin said.

Lucas wasn't surprised James had an escape plan. He wasn't going to get the chance to use it.

"Driving up now," Sera's voice murmured.

Lucas watched James pace across the barn's dirt floor. Stacks of hay bales were placed all over as if to create a maze. Colin sat on a chair near the barn doors, biting his nails. Was Colin nervous? Did that mean they knew what was coming? Was this an ambush?

"Someone's coming down the drive," one of Colin's men said, peeking through the crack in the barn door. "It looks like a woman. I don't see anyone else in the car."

James stopped pacing. "I knew that woman wasn't being truthful. She did receive our text."

"How do you know she didn't tell the marshal?" Colin grouched and without waiting for a reply said, "This is dumb. You're gonna get us killed."

Lucas was gratified to see a division in the ranks.

"Know your place," James said. "I could hand you over at any moment."

"And I can expose you," Colin shot back.

James flashed a smug smile. "No one will believe you. Now go bring the woman to me." James waved Colin away with a dismissive hand.

Colin grunted. "Can't I just kill the kid now?"

"You'll get your chance," James barked. "Now go."

Giving James a rude gesture, Colin rose and headed for the barn doors.

"Are you hearing this?" Lucas asked.

"We are," Gavin's voice said into his ear. "The minute Colin and those men walk out, we'll grab them. You secure Kenny."

Lucas hefted himself up and through the window, taking the rope with him. He dropped down onto the hayloft, thankful for the soft landing that covered any noise of his arrival. He peered over the hayloft railing.

James stood with his back to him. His back to Kenny.

So secure. The man was thinking he was safe. His arrogance would be his downfall.

Lucas swung over the hayloft railing and dropped down onto a hay bale next to Kenny. Lucas quickly placed a hand over the boy's mouth before he could make a sound to alert James and pulled Kenny into a crouch behind the hay bale.

Kenny's eyes grew wide with recognition, and he flung his arms around Lucas's torso.

In a low murmur, Lucas said, "Kenny, you're safe."

A figure loomed over them.

James held a SIG Sauer fitted with a noise suppressor in his hand.

Swiftly, Lucas maneuvered Kenny behind him to shield the boy. They would have to go through Lucas to reach the innocent target.

"Did you really think I didn't know your playbook? The lone wolf routine is going to be your downfall." James's voice shuddered through Lucas. "Stand up."

In Lucas's ear, he heard Duncan say, "Seven accounted for."

Rising to his feet, Lucas racked his brain to remember how many men were inside the barn with James. He didn't remember anyone saying a number. Was James alone? Lucas prepared to tackle his former boss when the SWAT command leader's voice came through the comm link in Lucas's ear saying, "Two new heat signatures."

Two men appeared from beneath infrared-resistant blankets. Each of them held AK-47s. Lucas gritted his teeth with frustration.

"You are a disgrace," Lucas said, hoping to buy time for those outside to breach the barn. "I trusted you. So many people trusted you."

James shrugged. "We all do what we have to do to survive."

Survive? Was the man serious? "You're the head of one of the country's most elite crime-fighting units."

"Yes, I am," James bragged. "And I also have one of the largest illegal weapons network this country has ever seen."

James just obliterated any doubt of a connection between him and Wayne. James was the man in charge. "Where are Adam Wayne and Eliza Mendez?"

His lip curling, James replied, "The rats skipped out. But they won't be able to outrun my network of operatives. Last I heard, they were in Costa Rica. Maybe they'll be bitten by a poisonous snake in the rainforest." Inside his ear, Lucas heard the SWAT command leader say, "Five seconds."

Lucas knew what that meant. They would breach.

Not waiting, Lucas pivoted and dropped to a crouch, wrapping his arms around Kenny and taking him to the floor of the barn behind the hay bale as the world around them exploded.

Gunfire ripped through the air. Screams punched through the sounds. Shouted orders followed.

Lucas's focus was on protecting the boy in his arms. Curling over him, Lucas's ears rang from all the racket.

Then someone touched his shoulder.

Startled, Lucas reared up with his weapon drawn.

Brian stood with his hands up in the air. His mouth moved,

but Lucas couldn't hear the words. He gave his head a shake to clear his ears. Slowly, the cacophony drained away and the normal sounds of the world returned.

Brian's muffled voice came through with, "All clear."

Relief seemed to drain Lucas of strength. He sat up and leaned back against the hay bale with Kenny clinging to him like a barnacle on a ship hull.

With Brian's help, Lucas stood, keeping his arms around the thin boy and shielding his face.

James's two men were down. Alive, but bleeding.

James was in handcuffs. FBI Special Agent in Charge Von Amici and FBI Agent McIntosh led James out of the barn.

With Brian leading the way, Lucas carried Kenny outside.

Kenny lifted his head and said, "I want my mommy."

"So do I, kid," Lucas muttered, referring to Paige. The woman he loved.

A chuckle sounded in Lucas's ear. He groaned aloud. He'd forgotten his team could still hear him. "Who's going to take us to Paige?"

Paige stared as a drip of condensation slid down the water bottle in front of her. She sat rooted on a barstool at the marble counter in the hotel suite's full-sized kitchen. Her heart hummed with anticipation. Word had come that Kenny was safe and on his way to the hotel. But nothing had been said about Lucas.

Was he okay? Was he bringing her son? What did the future hold for them?

Did she even want a future with Lucas?

A commotion at the front door brought her attention up and she held her breath. Brian, Gavin and Jace entered, scooping their wives up in joyous embraces.

Then Sera and Duncan walked in. Sera gave Paige a goofy grin and a wink.

Paige slid off the barstool as Aslan broke into a series of loud high-pitched happy barks and rushed toward the door.

Paige's eyes closed with joy. Kenny. He was alive and he was here. She opened her eyes and hurried toward the door just as Kenny shouted, "Mommy!"

Her son flung himself at her and she caught him, going to her knees as she openly wept and hugged her boy close. "Are you okay?"

"The cowboy saved me," Kenny said in a voice filled with awe.

Aslan danced around them, coming in for a lick and then dancing away.

Paige felt a presence at her side. She looked up to find Lucas standing there. His cowboy hat shaded the expression on his face. So handsome and kind and the type of man she could count on. A man to trust with her heart.

She lifted a hand from Kenny's shoulder and extended it to him.

Without hesitation, he took her hand and knelt beside her, wrapping her and Kenny in strong his arms.

"Thank you," she said to Lucas. "Does this mean we don't have to disappear into WITSEC?"

Next to her ear, he murmured, "No WITSEC. You're safe now. You can return to your life in Florida."

She drew away and reached up to push his cowboy hat back so she could see his eyes. "I don't want the past. I want a future. With you. Whatever that brings. If you'll have us."

She held her breath, waiting for him to respond. Had she made a mistake? Had she read him wrong? It didn't matter. She had to make him understand she loved him. "Lucas—"

Tenderly, he cupped her face. Tears glistened in his eyes. "Are you sure? I have a dangerous job. It wouldn't be fair—"

Her heart stuttered. "Life is filled with danger. Playing it safe isn't living."

A grin broke out on his handsome face. "Yes, I'll have you. If you'll have me."

"Yes, please," she managed past the exhilaration clogging her throat.

Lucas grinned. "Praise God above. I love you, Paige."

Heart bursting with joy, she murmured, "I love you, too, cowboy."

"Me, too!" Kenny yelled with enthusiasm.

Aslan barked as if to say "me, too."

Everyone in the room laughed and clapped.

Paige shared an embarrassed yet delighted smile with Lucas.

"You get all of us," he said sheepishly, gesturing to the four couples gawking at them.

Her love expanded to include his work family. "I'm good with that. And I can't wait to meet your other family and for you to meet my dad."

"We have a bright future ahead of us," he murmured.

In answer, she wound her arms around his neck and tugged him in for a kiss filled with promises and love.

* * * * *

If you enjoyed this story,
Don't miss the previous book,
Forced To Hide,
Available now from Love Inspired Suspense!

Discover more by Terri Reed at
LoveInspired.com

Dear Reader,

Thank you for coming on this journey with Paige and Lucas, the last book in my US Marshal series. When Lucas first appeared in the second book, *Forced to Hide*, I knew he had to have his own story. Pairing him with a widow and her son, pushed him out of his comfort zone. Being put on protection detail rather than the more active fugitive pursuits that he preferred forced him to take stock of his life and realize he wanted more. Paige had been hurt in the past and trust didn't come easy for her. But trust is earned, and Lucas definitely earned her trust.

I hope you enjoyed their romance as they dodged bullets and mayhem and finally obtained their joyful ending. And it was so fun to bring back characters from the three previous books to help Lucas and Paige. We all need friends who have our backs.

For more information about me and my books, visit my webpage at www.terrireed.com.

I'd love for you to sign up for my newsletter and receive updates on upcoming releases.

Until we meet again,
Terri Reed